Vol. 2

BREVITY IN
PARADISE

OC WRITERS GUILD

20 — 19

The stories and poetry included in this anthology are works of fiction. The names, characters, places and incidents are products of the writers' imaginations or have been used fictitiously to give a sense of authenticity and are not to be construed as real. Any resemblance to persons living or dead, actual events, locales or organizations is purely coincidental.

Cover and group portrait photography, Jim Topping
Cover typography and typesetting, Ris Fleming-Allen
Introduction, Anita Grazier

ISBN 9781082105821

Printed by KDP, Amazon.com

*For our friends and families who
send us off to the library to dream
a bit every Saturday morning.*

*And for the Bristol Farms Cafe staff who
know our orders and wonder where the
heck we are when meetings run late.*

Introduction

A writer is a curious animal. With nothing more than an overheard remark in a supermarket to stimulate his thoughts, a writer can create a sketch of an imaginary person or a word picture of an exotic land. When you get a bunch of talented writers together each week and present them with a prompt of a few words, they can produce an enormous variety of stories and poems, and each piece will be as unique as the author.

This has been the premise of OC Writers Guild for more than a decade. The word prompts are the beginning; the camaraderie of the group provides the continuum, and the end result is some fine writing.

Here is a collection of work from OCWG. Choose a story, find a comfortable place to read…and enjoy!

Anita Grazier

Table of Contents

SPRING

SUMMER

FALL

WINTER

SPRING

LITERARY FICTION

Coming of Age

Christine O'Connor

As the gusting winds cut through my brand new, too-thin-for-the-outdoors uniform, I stood shivering at the bus stop, watching the young cherry trees rearing and pawing like frightened horses trying to throw their riders. I was waiting, but not very patiently, for the ever-late 53 bus.

It was the kind of March morning where the thin spring sunlight offers no competition to the blasts of the chill northern wind: a wind that is still the child of winter. The Greenwich Borough Council had corralled a string of cherry saplings that stretched along the sidewalk. Each tree was staked and tethered, with its roots held in place by a black iron grate encircling its trunk.

By the time the bus came, my teeth were chattering and I was chilled to the bone and terrified of being late. But lessons are learned in the most obscure of ways and I was in awe of those young trees; for despite the wind whipping and tearing at their branches, it never ever severed those tiny, unfurled pink buds from the slim silver boughs.

Fortunately, I made it in time to clock on for the early morning shift. At eighteen years of age and just recently graduated, it doesn't do to be late on your first day. I met Mary Millar on that first day in the Assisted Living Facility and in the 40 years since, I have never forgotten her. Whenever the first buds bloom on the cherry trees in my own garden I think of her. She was not unlike a cherry tree with her delicate pink complexion, glossy silver-white hair and long graceful neck. Hers was a rare sort of beauty, not at all what you would expect to find among the wrinkled and aging population of a Borough-run elder care facility in South East London.

The building itself (back then we called it a Home) was nothing to write home about. It was a single story 1960s structure, one small step in London's post war reconstruction. Nearby, unremarkable blocks of public housing climbed upwards, testament to the prevailing architectural fashion for low budget functionalism. What was surprising was that despite the otherwise dreary urban landscape, New Charlton House was surrounded by a lawn so perfect and green that even the boldest of dandelions would never have dared to show its head.

Inside the Home, aside from the strikingly large photograph of Councilor Sharp presiding over its opening ceremony, there was nothing fancy. It was much like its occupants, the ordinary folk who hailed from the neighborhood and lived out their lives in the shadow of that Other London. Down here, down river in the old docklands, there were no palaces or fancy parades, just the workaday London that tourists never see.

There was little that was lovely outside the Home and even less in the lives of the residents, so it was a surprise, as my supervisor showed me around, to catch a glimpse of Mary Millar amongst all that ordinariness. Even the drab hues of her faded wing chair flattered her, like the muted background of the Mona Lisa. Mary was a spectacularly lovely woman with long dark eyelashes surrounding cornflower-blue eyes. She sat facing the west window, composed and almost posed in Madonna-like serenity, shrouded in a white walled, green-tiled utilitarian care home.

Beyond the window, there was an inviting bank of grass, but the old folks seldom got to walk or sit there: it was too steep for stiff old legs to climb on their own. Although the doors at the front of the Home were never locked, few of the residents ever went far or ventured out into the great beyond. Going outside of those doors was like going beyond the Pale. It was very rare when their visitors ever took them outside, let alone took them out for the day.

Whenever people are trapped indoors, the view from the window becomes their only link with the outside world. The gusting wind or Jack Frost on the windowpane is news. It's something to talk about, and more particularly something to share. We talked a lot about the plants outside and studied the progress of the cherry trees, from spring buds to summer green and back to bare-limbed winter. And I learned that it is only when the blossoms have faded that their frail resilience is broken. It is then and only then that they fall from the tree.

On my first day my first task was to wheel the cart round to the various lounges to serve the morning coffee and biscuits. Mary sat in her chair, silent, straight-backed and elegant. She smiled and I thought how dignified old age could be. It was a shock when I compared her to some of the other residents in that lounge, the senile who muttered to themselves and the drooling lop-sided stroke victims propped up by their pillows. They were the archetypes of how our old age can be.

I set Mary Millar's coffee on the table beside her and started to help the ones who could no longer eat or drink by themselves, trying to think of the residents as I thought of my own grandmother. I passed from one chair to the next, straightening crochet blankets over bony knees, passing out more biscuits and passing the time of day.

Old folks are perkier in the morning; it's in the afternoons that they doze off. I was a new face, so as I handed out the coffee, they asked all about me—who I was, where I lived and was I married. A few told me about themselves, others gossiped about their fellow residents, telling me far more than I ever wanted to know. Several took real pride in telling me that Mary "used to sing in the Opera at Covent Garden, before her surgery," and invited me to come in one evening and listen to her sing.

Then I heard all about Charlie, whom I had yet to meet. With a bit of a wink one lady warned me that "I'd best take Charlie wiv a pinch of salt, luv, cos he's a bit of a tease." He was also, so I gleaned, "a dab 'and on the old joanna; leastways he was, till 'e 'ad a stroke."

Later at lunchtime, not being a Londoner, I had to ask Peggy for a translation. She smiled, nodded at the piano and with a twinkle in her eye mystified me even further, telling me that when Charlie was in the mood he used to play for hours and "they'd 'ave a bit of a knees- up."

When I returned some time later to pick up the cups, Mary's coffee was cold and her biscuits untouched. She sat there in her chair, gazing at the window and smiling toward the street. I assumed that she was watching the neighborhood children who loved to roll and slide down the grassy bank, collecting massive grass stains on their clothes as they laughed and shrieked. It hadn't occurred to me that I needed to feed her.

The next day Peggy, my tall thin supervisor with blacker than black dyed hair, seven grown children and a stack of worldly wisdom, told me to go and wake up the residents in the Mobility Unit. One of the mysterious things about elder care is that euphemisms are rampant. In the Memory Unit everybody has lost theirs, and in the Mobility Unit all the residents were bed ridden or wheelchair bound. Nowadays we'd be called Certified Nursing Assistants, but back then when there was no certificate, we were just care assistants, and Peggy made the morning duty roster sound easy

"Give 'em their morning cuppa, pop them on the commode, put a bowl of warm water on the nightstand and give 'em a quick once over."

But as always, Peggy shared the extra flourishes that put the care into being a care assistant. It was the gift of a little extra time. At first I was terrified when I had to shave the men, afraid of slitting somebody's throat. But safety razors and an old man's tough skin are a big help. At Peggy's prompting I also discovered that a hot towel, a quick dash of aftershave and a friendly pat on an elderly cheek can make an old man's day.

With my ladies I spent a bit more time on their hair, and the spritz of perfume made a world of difference. The care assistants were usually too rushed to spend much time on an individual, but as I discovered, when people have lived beyond any future, it is the simple pleasures in the present that can bring great joy.

Sometimes the Duty Nurse would bawl me out if my charges were late for breakfast. I apologized but never did tell her that from the residents' perspective, it was well worth skipping a bit of their everyday breakfast routine. It shouldn't really be surprising that a dab of moisturizer massaged into a withered cheek can bring a real flush of pleasure and an added glow.

There was no doubt about it, Mary was different. Compared to the wrinkled leathery skins of most of the residents, she looked like a child. I supposed that she must be in her 60s since she'd been in the Home for nearly ten years. Later I was told that she was brought in when she was a lot younger; she had never recovered from the anesthetic for some minor surgery. Her cheeks were still smooth and pink and even the few laugh lines around her eyes flattered her. There was no artifice about her looks; she wore no makeup and she had never been near a plastic surgeon.

Mary's hair was different too. Most of the residents had their hair cut short and straight. It was easier for us; quick to comb and easy to wash. We were always too short staffed to do much else. Mary's hair was short too, but it was blunt cut and beautifully shaped. Her niece came in regularly on her half day from the salon. Mary's hair was stunning, stylish and simple; a soft silky white frame to the perfect oval of her smiling face.

It is important to keep the elderly clean and free from sores. This is difficult when they are incontinent, so a bath is an important aspect of their daily routine. For those who were unable or too unstable to get into a bathtub, we used a hoist that looked like it was designed to dunk a medieval witch.

When we bathed Mary I was surprised that we needed the hygiene sling, she looked so fit. She was slim and lean, without a hint of arthritis and her skin was smooth and taught. There were a few stretch marks and the soft dark line beneath her navel that was the hallmark of her motherhood. But she was like a willing child, smiling but saying nothing.

Afterwards we dressed Mary in a cornflower blue lamb's wool dress that matched the color of her eyes; her daughter always bought her beautiful clothes. Mary looked so radiant that I complimented her, thinking that perhaps she was shy of being bathed by a stranger, but she said nothing. I took her back to the sitting room and settled her in the chair facing the window.

Except for the flowers and grass outside, the view from the West Wing wasn't up to much. The neighboring flats were built on land cleared of the burned, bombed out streets of terraced houses that crisscrossed their way down to the river Thames. They were the houses that had once been homes for many of our residents before the doodlebugs and V2s obliterated their landscape forever. In the far distance the tall soot-blackened brick chimneys of Woolwich power station stood tall, proud and unbowed by the successive German air raids.

Despite the distinct unloveliness of the general neighborhood, the grounds of the Home were the pride and joy of Jimmy the gardener. He was older than some of our residents, had a ready smile and was always bringing in bouquets or a rose for somebody's birthday. Jimmy worked as much for love of gardening as for the money, for there was never a season in that garden without bright blossoms or foliage or berries. He radiated joy because he was a man with his health, his strength and most of all, his independence.

Sometimes we care assistants, the ones with no medical training, were sent over to the Skilled Nursing Wing if they were short-staffed. As a trainee I wasn't asked to go over there at first, but sometimes when Peggy came back it was with a frown and she would mutter:

"The nurses over there are too high and mighty to do what's right for the poor buggers," and at the time, I didn't understand.

People end up in Assisted Living for many reasons, but seldom by choice. There were some who recognized that they could no longer care for themselves. They were the happiest, accepting their lot and often grateful for the care that we gave them. Others did not get to choose what was effectively their incarceration. It seems to me now that there is perhaps a small blessing inherent in the fading of a memory.

It is a time of life when time can be blurred and days blend into each other, a stage where present and past are no longer regulated by the day of the week or month in the year. These were the residents who cheerfully looked forward to the next visit, to Johnny who "was coming soon" or

Jackie "would be visiting next week." Sometimes residents would ask me to read their letters and I would read that same letter to them, week after week. It seemed like their faltering minds and forgetfulness actually shielded them from the pain of their daily reality. Mostly their loved ones were dead and the live ones who were left would never be coming.

As for Mary it was remarkable that, unresponsive as she was, she was surrounded by love. Her daughter dropped in several times a week and her sailor son visited whenever he was on leave. One day I walked into the lounge and noticed a lovely young woman sitting next to Mary. From the resemblance between them she had to be Mary's daughter. She sat close to her mother, giving her a manicure. I watched her as she held Mary's hands with a tenderness that was almost painful to see, shaping her nails and painting them a soft, pretty pink.

Susie Millar Smith came every Sunday to bring the grandchildren. Every week the two fair-haired little girls brought a gift for Mary and every week amused themselves unwrapping it for her and then helping their "Nan" to eat her chocolates.

Others in the Home were not so lucky. They were the aunts and uncles and parents who were put away, out of sight and out of mind, discarded like old broken toys. These were often the most difficult to work with. Sometimes, if anger and frustration got the better of them they would lash out at us with a gnarled fist or wrinkled hand. Peggy did warn me, yet she almost apologized for them because, "They're away with the fairies, they can't 'elp themselves."

There was one resident whom I remember very well, perhaps because of her name. Betty Sharp, mother of the Councilor, was one of the unwanted elderly, an inconvenience to her politically ambitious son and her daughter-in-law's busy social agenda. Betty was a sharp dresser, always wearing beautifully tailored but well-worn tweeds. She absolutely insisted upon keeping her hair long, and except for washing it, which she could no longer do herself, would let nobody touch it. She brushed it a hundred times every morning then pulled it back into a tight gray-streaked bun.

Betty was perfectly though painfully self-sufficient, forcing her arthritic fingers to do up her blouse buttons and despite the pain in her hips, always insisted on walking, scorning a wheelchair. I was impressed by her independence and perplexed when Peggy warned me to tread warily with "her ladyship."

She kept a large silver framed photograph of her son by her bedside and frequently told us how well he was doing or when he bought a new house or car. Betty took pride in reading to anybody who would listen to the articles in the local newspaper about her son, Councilor Sharp: but he seldom came to visit. It was only twice that I knew of, in the whole year.

Betty Sharp, as I said, was aptly named and of all of our residents she most resented being in the Home. I felt sorry for her. One morning she seemed to be in a friendly mood and told me that before the arthritis crippled her fingers she'd been a music teacher. I made a little joke about B. Sharp being a good name for a music teacher and was surprised and rather irked when she snapped that I was being "thoroughly impertinent." I apologized and asked if she would like me to help her down the stairs. By way of reply she hissed in a tone of pure distilled venom, that "she wouldn't be needing any help from her maid."

Mary had been in the Home for nearly ten years, and Betty for at least three, but death in a Care home is an inevitability. Charlie the old soldier and much decorated war hero was the first to go, just a few weeks after I started work there. He was a tall man with crinkly gray hair, and despite his stroke-withered arm he walked ram-rod straight till a few days before he died. In his whole life he never ever conceded to the pain in his bullet-shattered knees. He even joked, sometimes, suggesting that "being at the wrong end of a Maxim gun was never a good idea."

Charlie had a smile for everybody, a line for all the women, and a South Londoner's wicked sense of humor. If anybody complained about their aches and pains, he'd flash them a grin and make some outrageous remark. One of his favorites was:

"If you keep moaning like that, luv, I'll take you to the vets and get you put down."

Yet crazy as it seemed, his outrageousness made the old folks laugh. They loved him, and it was magic to see how easily he could convert a scowl into a smile.

Sometimes though, in his quieter moments when I shaved him in the mornings, he'd tell me about his wife of forty years and their son who were killed in the Blitz. He fretted about them because he felt as if he betrayed them when he couldn't visit their graves any more.

One morning after I had been working at the Home for a few weeks, the Charge Nurse summoned me into her office to tell me that Charlie had suffered another stroke and had been transferred to the Skilled Nursing Unit. She asked me to go over there and "prepare him." I suppose I must have looked completely blank because there was a pause and in a gentler voice than her usual commanding tone she said:

"If Charlie's your first, you'd better wait for Peggy."

I knew nothing of the practicalities of dying: that people close to death still need to be kept clean; that soiled bed linens have to be changed without disturbing them; that nails need to be cut and men's stubble shaved because they will continue to grow a bit, post mortem.

Charlie lay in his bed perfectly still, talking to those that I could not see. Peggy handed me the nail scissors. His hands and feet were ice cold to touch. It was hard to cut through his thick, ridged nails. It was only then that I understood what Peggy had meant a few weeks before when she said that "we need to do right for the poor buggers." This time around it was my turn and although he was "my first," I was determined that I would "do right" for Charlie.

Soon after I finished shaving him, Charlie started to sing old tunes from the Thirties and Forties. He sang on and on for the rest of day and through into the night. The following morning we shaved him again, and at noon he died.

That evening, for the first time, I was offered the chance to work some overtime, so I stayed at the Home for the night shift. At eight o'clock when it was nearing sundown, I took a break. As I sat in the staffroom drinking my tea, I was astonished to hear the Ave Maria sung in warm, rich lyrical tones. At first I thought it was a radio playing, and when I walked out into the corridor to listen, I realized that the haunting soprano voice was coming from the West Wing.

I walked toward where the sound seemed to be coming from and found Peggy stopping to listen, too. I peaked in, over her shoulder. Mary Millar stood in front of her chair facing the west window and bathed in the red glow from the evening sunset, singing Schubert's Ave Maria.

All day long, year in and year out, Mary never spoke a word. She smiled, but knew nobody; she was serene and she was gentle and someone would have to feed her and bathe her and diaper her for the rest of her life. Her beautiful eyes were empty eyes and it was a frightening thought, if the eyes are the windows to the soul. Yet, although the doctors and psychologists could never explain it, every night at sundown Mary would stand and sing Ave Maria with a passion and a rare beauty in her voice.

My children are grown now, and even my grandchildren are stretching and strengthening their wings before they fly from the nest. Sometimes as I look at them, aware that I am creeping towards old age, I think of Mary Millar. I thought her old back then, when I worked in the care home. But now, with the passing of my own years I realize the full extent of her tragedy. A gifted, beloved and beautiful woman, barely into middle age: she was unable to live her life to the full and unable to die.

I wonder now about her, how long she continued to sit in the corner of that lounge, lost in her timeless existence, or if at last, like the cherry trees in spring, the bloom has faded and the petals withered and dropped.

Existential Socks

Jennifer Hedgecock

I

On the nightstand sits a half empty bottle of gin, the screw cap left abandoned on the dresser; the reading lamp is still on next to the unmade bed, the drapes closed, obscuring the afternoon sun. Dirty clothes lie on the bathroom floor. On the pillow is a letter in block writing, a salutation with a few lines about things in life that people try to sort out for others when they don't really know what it means themselves. Maid service enters the room, using disinfectant to disguise the stale odor of booze and cigarette smoke. The woman renting the room is past middle age, short cropped grey hair, rail thin. She pays in cash one week in advance.

The desk clerk, Emma, is a local high school student who spends the evening shift studying for her classes, and cannot help notice the woman in room twenty-three, her hands so delicate, yet agile, the skin untouched by age or harsh weather, perfectly smooth, as if they did not belong to that old woman filling out personal data on the motel guest forms with her current address and emergency information. This woman is unlike the others who come and go through that rundown motel in Truckee where Interstate 80 connects to Lake Tahoe, to Sacramento, to the Donner Pass. It is an intersection where nothing hap-pens, where tourists or drifters travel through either east or west. During the winter, people book a room because the roads are closed, and they have nowhere to go. They show up without a reservation, hoping for something, just for the night, or until the storm passes. For now, it is late fall, no snow in the mountains yet, no skiing, and this woman arrives late afternoon alone, asking about the cost for a room, wearing a plaid shirt and loose fitting jeans. Her watery blue eyes dart curiously around the lobby. She speaks in a deep commanding voice inconsistent with her small physical form.

Startled by the woman's tone, Emma adjusts her posture from a slouch to an upright position. Oddly the teen-age desk clerk admires the woman's effortless mien of superiority and independence. In contrast Emma's mother and her mother's friends are high school dropouts and work minimum wage paying jobs, their children raising one another because mom works second shifts. But Emma finds a charming eccentricity in the woman.

Legally she isn't suppose to be working these hours, but Emma takes whatever shift she can get, putting away money for things like books and college, saving for a dream that is out of reach. She walks home after work, the smell of fresh pine needles leading her to a trailer park a mile away, where her mother's boyfriend slams the door behind him, her two kid brothers, from different fathers, run through the cramped spaces. They are "those" kinds of people, her family. She fears that she will become one of them. They talk differently, smell different than some of the people she meets at the motel who travel from far away places.

A pile of dishes lie in the sink, chili and cheddar cheese caked on one plate, egg yolk forming a solid yellow patch on another. She stares at the mess, then grabs her house keys swinging open the screen door that she had just entered. Maybe she can sleep in one of the empty guest rooms at the motel or stay in the girls locker room at her high school.

II

About a week after checking in, the woman leaves at 8:23 p.m. on a Thursday night. Before going out, she passes by Emma at the front desk, and pays no attention to the girl, neither speaking nor looking at her. Because she is now use to these gestures, Emma stops taking it personally. When she finishes her shift in the early hours the following day, the woman never returns. Maybe she went out to dinner or got stuck somewhere. But by late after-noon, the woman is found lying in a parking lot behind a dumpster, her eyes glassy and staring at the sky, her hand grasping, clutching onto something invisible. The police aren't sure what happened.

The brother of the woman arrives the next day, early evening, to claim his sister's personal effects. They look alike, the gaunt face, the seriousness in those watery blue eyes. Emma volunteers to take the night shift on the weekend, and so she greets the brother, trying to talk to him, though she doesn't really know what to say.

"Who was she?"

"A doctor. Cornell graduate." He pauses looking across the front desk at this teenage girl while handing her his identification.

"She was one of two recipients of the American Heart Association Awards," he explains in a steady voice. Emma bites her lower lip staring at him in an awkward attempt to find his sister looking back at her.

"Oh?" answers Emma, then copying down his name and address in the registration book, she is too timid to look up again. Cornell. One of those schools on the East Coast where rich people send their kids. You have to be really smart to go to that school. Even if you do have money, she thinks. God.

When she reads the paper later that week, it reports that the man's sister died from a seizure, that she was intoxicated, and this was later followed by hypothermia. She was sixty-two. Her name was Alice. Her family lived in Minnesota but originally came from south-ern California. Sixty-two?

III

Alice had been walking around Truckee, everywhere. She had taken a bus up near the crest of the Sierra Nevada, after selling her motorcycle, selling the car, and losing the house. And now she just walked with her backpack that was sometimes a little too heavy, and that was when it was time to check in somewhere. Maybe for a day, maybe for two nights. Not sure. So tired. It wasn't the weight of the backpack. It wasn't the long hikes. It was not her hot sticky clothes in early summer through late fall. Instead it was the weight of a heavy mind. Why so warm? She could walk and walk. But she felt better setting down her backpack, gazing off into something no one else could see. It was jumping into a part of the lake, or standing beneath the waterfall, her nakedness relieved by the cold water against her skin, that cooled the mind. She loved smelling fresh pine, right up there in the mountains, the blue sky, and she would squint hard looking up to find some-thing in the air that might be missing. But it was just blue and pure, like when she lived in Wyoming for a while near Cody and would come outside to her ranch, just to press her face against the body of her horse, to breath in the life of that animal so warm and calm, which made her feel untroubled inside. And she missed those days, looking for some cloud pattern in the sky that might resemble her horse that she ached for so much. She smiled, that unbreakable real smile because it felt good to remember. But why did she lose the horse? Then it started coming back, and that made her look away from the sky, to stop looking for that something, and just stare ahead and keep walking. Don't look at the sky. Don't think about Wyoming. Just don't think. Is there a way not to think? No. She tried that for many years, especially the last year when she worked at the hospital in Chicago and had to admit to herself, in just a tiny moment of lucidity, when a thought came that made sense, that this life was over, at least this part. The memory shaped an image of herself, so starched and perfect in an expensive grey suit, sitting behind a mahogany desk in her office and looking behind her at the view of Lake Michigan on a cloudy day. It was coming to an end, and so it did. So many endings came in the last ten years. When would those endings stop? Not with the sky, not with the ranch, not with the long walk south-west away from the shore of the river, and not with those existential socks she wore that kept her feet moving in a direction going nowhere.

The stereo was blaring "A Whiter Shade of Pale", the song on repeat, growing bigger with a thundering noise that drowned out the sound in her head, the bottle of wine almost empty, and she sat on her bed, leaning forward, staring at that damn armoire. What to do with it? Toss it she thought. Besides, it belonged to him. Well they actually picked it out together. She liked the wood, strong and sturdy while he commented on the design work, the fact that it would be around long after forever, even after the two of them. She smiled to herself, thinking about this, then frowned over the regret of remembering that time. "I think I can move it. Moved furniture like this before," and she lifted herself up, pushing the heavy piece from side to side, inching it closer to the door. She had to pause in be-tween just to catch her breath, and at a certain point, she even relit her cigarillo, taking one long drag, then crushing it out in the ashtray she had cleaned earlier that day. By the time she reached the stairs that went down to the front door, she became more confused. "How do I get this down the steps?" The music blasted, "cartwheels across the floor" and "feeling seasick." Yes this is the hard part, about us somewhere in that heavy furniture. But she figured she could inch it carefully down the steps the same way she moved it out of the bedroom; she just wouldn't take any breaks, and that would be fine. But it didn't go fine, and it wasn't until the next day that she woke up at the bottom of the staircase, lying on broken pieces of the armoire, part of it on top of her, crushing what was left of her, with nothing much left inside. Her leg felt twisted, the circulation somewhat cut off, and her head throbbed; she wondered how she ever gained consciousness from this, trying to crawl out from underneath it. Most of the armoire was now in pieces, though it ironically lessened her fall down the stairs. The music was still going. Oh yeah, she thought. Repeat, repeat. She went into the bathroom, checking her face in the mirror. A big gash had formed just above her hairline. It was too late for stitches. "Just have to heal on its own," she thought.

IV

Video cameras at the quickie mart record her that night where she collapses behind the dumpster. The brother wants to see the tapes. He just has to know. All these bits and pieces left behind might tell more about the sister he lost even before she was gone, the woman who never hesitated to take long road trips riding along the coast on her Harley Davidson. Oh where did she go?

The store manager rewinds the tape. The video is in black and white, with a blue tinted streak, and no sound. It shows the parking lot with only one car, a Toyota Corolla that belongs to the cashier working that night. Alice leaves the store, a paper bag in hand, and the camera only shows her back. But it is definitely her, short hair, blue jeans, skinny. The camera follows her out the door until she rounds the corner. The manager stops the tape, takes it out, and puts another one into the video player. The camera now faces out into the rear parking lot with a view of the dumpster, the trees lining the street which fall off into a mountainous terrain, still in black and white with that blue tint. Alice falls down like a boxer receiving a knockout punch. No movement, no sign of life, no calling out for help. Her face appears to be pressed into the concrete. It is October in Truckee and 28 degrees. The tape continues like this for four minutes and twenty-eight seconds until Al-ice attempts to pull herself up in a push up position, moving her legs, but she collapses again, and lays there rolling on her side. She makes another effort, pulling herself up on her elbows, her eyes shut, squinting. But again she collapses and this time her limbs start shaking impulsively. Alice makes no more attempts to pull herself up, the blue tint on the screen reinventing itself as something different, the landscape changing, as the brother stands watching the video tape, watching his sister as she dies. Her body goes into another seizure. Cardiac arrest. Then she stops moving, everything is still, the room where he stands is still, not a sound.

Inside her motel room, there is a receipt for $40.97 cents, but it does not show the con-tents of her items that she bought, it just gives the date, time and expense, October 21 at 11:08 p.m., Wednesday night. He wanted really badly to know what she bought. He wanted to know whether she bought another bottle. Cigarettes. All the items meant to dull the pain.

V

She fell all the time, suffering from problems with brain injury. The headaches were the worst. The ranch out in Wyoming let her get up when she wanted, go to bed when she wanted. But she couldn't sleep and would pace around the house, around and around, searching for things that she had lost or thought were gone. Carter called the first year she moved in.

"Are you still in Chicago?"

"I am. Just, uh. Well. I don't know. Wanted to know how you are."

She chuckled, that raw throaty laugh. "I'm fine babe. All is fine. I take it you're still at the hospital."

"Yup. Probably not missing much."

She did not answer, and he found himself struggling to say all the things that he meant to tell her before he called. Come back. Come back here. I can help you. We can try again. Maybe there's something else we haven't looked into. Let's just give it go.

But there was no go, and he could sense that she was already getting restless, holding that receiver, waiting for him to say something, the feelings that cannot be communicated in words, and the fact that even if she could feel them, she would never respond. So he asked about all the other things that don't matter, the weather, her new home, the lake running next to her house. Was anyone there to help on the ranch? But she made this even more difficult responding with the short answers that did not permit him to take those questions to a whole other level. So like two lovers who still care about each other and can no longer make sense of the life that they have chosen, they said their good-byes, and hung up. He sat for a long time, staring at the television, the sound muted, while he tried to imagine her in that great big house where she was living, so far away from the city, from other people who were sick in different ways from her, from the miles and miles that now kept them apart, those rolling hills, flat arid land covered with ice, the highway that people traveled so frequently, anxious to be wherever they needed to go.

Before she left Chicago, Alice warned him that they shared only a prison together. She wanted to go on living after she got out of prison. Her eyes glistened with specks of grey and blue, a big smile on her face when she confessed this to him. A prison. He could never be free. He'd always think of the way she said those words. How does someone create an escape route from the very prison of which they manifest all on their own? Can they every really leave?

They met at a party. It was the second year of med school, and she seldom went out, quiet usually, but not because she was shy or had nothing to say. Her mind was never on pause, and she could sit there coolly among her peers, without any notion of anxiety or stress. He watched her, studied her many times in class. But the surprise came when he saw her on a Saturday night outside of class, surrounded by other students, and sitting Indian style in the middle of the room. She was drinking a beer and smoking a joint. Her hair was long then, thick and dark blond, bluer eyes, and she had that California thing about her going strong, long limbs, real thin, but not frail. Sometimes you could see the veins in her cheeks, especially when she talked with excitement about something that mattered to her. She also didn't seem to care about anything except school. She didn't care about what she wore to class or how she wore it. Sometimes she even forgot to shower. She could only pay attention to one thing and it wasn't parties, or socializing, or men, or marriage, or even anything having to do with right now. It was always about school, medicine, being the first to know the right answer to something, looking at the study of the heart in ways that no one else had attempted. She could look other students right in the eye and see into their soul. It made people uncomfortable, men especially. Other women did not care for her much and maybe the only one who did was her sister. But they respected her. When she talked, she annunciated each word clearly because she wanted to be heard. When she thought someone wasn't listening, she repeated herself, saying each word more slowly, more carefully. She wanted people to know what those words meant and in what order. So even though she was sitting there at that party so casual like, a little drunk and a little stoned, the part of her rational mind remained unchanged. If she was at all vulnerable at that moment, Carter wanted to see it and know it because he felt so vulnerable himself sitting next to her.

At that party, he pushed his way through a dense crowd just to get to Alice, and he sat in mock Indian style with her. She would not look over. He had to do something to win her attention, to earn her respect, her trust, and that was how it should be. The two of them. She wasn't impressed by smart people, she was moved by honest people, those who spoke the truth and followed it up in what they did. Carter and Alice talked at the party about the upcoming election, and she was voting for McGovern. "An extremist, liberal? You're serious?" She responded with a sideways glance, raising an eyebrow, an expression that came to define the shape of their relationship in years to come. He could not play the tough guy, the guy who must hide his feelings. He couldn't pretend that things really didn't matter. He could not disguise his affection for her. To do so would have made her less real.

When Carter first asked her to marry him, they had known each other for eight years. He loved her, but she could go off in these passionate tempers. Over time he discovered that it was better to say nothing. Just let her exhaust herself until she was so worn down, she could say and do no more. Most people might call them rages, but he decided on a different term: passions. She was filled with passion when she talked with disdain about simple minded hospital administrators, more concerned with budget cuts than quality care. Her mind, was a tunnel that moved in a linear way where she sought corresponding links from point A to point B. She argued that an answer was always there, it would present itself with the right kind of work, strategy. So she would spend hours trying to work it out in her head, going over the paperwork on something, studying the chart of one of her patients, taking a look at the nature of certain disorders to discover something that had only been speculative. Though she may have found answers, they always came at a cost. One of the administrators tried getting her fired when she had only been in Chicago for two years.

Alice hated the city. She was from the west coast, grown up along the beaches of south-ern California, surfing with her brother and sister, snorkeling, scuba diving out by Catalina Island, the night dives. So she was never a windy city girl. But she loved the hospital, all its potential, its research facility, the patients, some of the most daring cases. She loved the challenge, and since she was always at work, she didn't have to be reminded that she lived in Chicago.

She had that other kind of passion, when her whole body seemed to reawaken, like when she saw the Philharmonic orchestra perform Sibelius, or when she went motorcycle riding across country with her younger brother, or when she was out there on one of the night dives, because the marine life was far different at that hour, more exotic.

Carter tried reaching her one more time that year while she was still in Wyoming, but there was no answer. The line had been disconnected. That was not unexpected. She would often cancel phone services, or forget to pay the bill, or move suddenly without any sign of where she might be going. He remarried a new, younger woman whose love was not of the same intensity that he shared with Alice, but had its own kind of spark. Seven years later, Carter got a call from Alice's brother.

"I'm really sorry. I felt like you needed to know."

"What happened?"

"She's just gone. You know how it was."

Carter said nothing and hung up the phone, sitting there, the choking feeling where the world is in suspension, and the only person in the room who can feel that it stopped actually wants to go on living but is stuck in a bowl of glue. He tried to figure out what he felt, and really, it was not sadness, or loss. He had felt that way so many times over the years, even the last time they parted, when she was drunk and in a bad passion, and forced him out of the house, and then woke up in the hospital because she had fallen over the banister and almost died. He felt sad then, he felt the loss of her over and over, a powerful cycle that kept him spinning out of control, running after her in a circle, with this glaring light above them, always over them and he could never quite catch her, not when she fell that time, the other times, not when she lost control of herself, not when she drank, not when she disappeared somewhere, not when she left the hospital. Two weeks after that phone call, her brother sent him a couple of her things in the mail, including her commencement announcement, her name noted with honors at graduation from Cornell, the old image of the woman he had wanted to marry years ago. The only thing he knew that day when he hung up the phone with her brother was that he wanted to go on living when he got out of that prison, and today was the first day that he was finally free. She had finally set him free.

The Past Is Never Dead

Jennifer Hedgecock

Thetford Priory, where the Virgin Mary was spotted several times during the 12th century, was open year round without a fee. One of the most important monasteries in England was in ruins with moss covered walls of flint and stone still standing. My sister and I liked going in the mornings during the Fall season, roaming around in the light fog and misty air, disturbing some private ritual among the ghosts gathered together. I don't remember being allowed to ride our bicycles through the abbey, or my sister's Big Wheel throwing dust along the pebbled footpath. But we ignored the rules. When we were bored and my mother had had enough of us, we went to the Priory, entering through a gate in the residential part of our neighborhood. Located near the entrance was a large house belonging to the abbey, that looked more like a haunted mansion. Making up stories, I told my sister that an old woman lived there by herself and watched us when we played on the grounds. I'm not sure she believed me, but I always convinced myself that the stories I made up were true, picturing a mysterious woman not quite so old but with white, grey hair worn in a bun, like the one my great-grandmother wore years before she went into a nursing home, when the staff clipped her hair into a crew cut, as if her womanhood had been chopped off as well, her once plump body, now bone-thin. I modeled this make-believe woman after my great-grandmother, a fleshy woman, an ultra lean woman, who rarely smiled. The woman in my imagination wore a full length black dress, long sleeved, and a black veil so transparent I could make out the lines around her grey blue eyes. I always expected a hearse to be parked outside that house, ready to carry one of our cold bodies away, should it come down to that.

My sister usually ran ahead of me whenever we went to the abbey, expecting me to follow her. We were different in age, alike in our features, and different in hair color. My younger sister had white blond hair, like gold. I believed that if she ever cut her hair like my great-grandmother, that her golden locks could be spun into coins. I liked brushing her hair, and she knew this, so she would keep it from me, sometimes bribing me for my allowance, and some-times, I would make a counter-offer, proposing a ride on my bicycle. But we always reached an impasse, wanting more than what the other was willing to give.

When we went to the priory, we climbed all over the ruins. Sticking to the path was never fun, and though my sister was five years younger than me, she always braved climbing the highest wall inside the ruins, running ahead of me, her elbows pointing outwards, her legs knee knocked, the funniest sprint I ever saw. Usually we wore our rain slickers because it was England, and although it wasn't raining when we left the house that day, it would start at some point, and we found shelter underneath the hoods of our coats. A worse fear than getting wet, was returning home to our mother who would decide to keep us indoors the rest of the day.

Sometimes we hunted ghosts, and we were certainly in the right place to do that sort of thing because it was a known fact that the Thetford Priory was haunted. Ghosts do not just come out at night. We could feel them with us in broad daylight, sometimes touching our shoulders, sneaking up behind us or just getting damn irritated with our noise, running through the abbey with no supervision and yelling because it was so much fun to do so. I think ghosts sometimes don't like children because they cannot join us in our amusement. But the past is never dead; it lives right along with us, darting in and out of secret corners, catching us off guard, poking fun of us when we think we're too important. When it did rain, and my sister and I sat side by side on one of the abbey walls bombed by the Germans, we could feel one of those ghosts sitting next to us because he was lonely and wanted us to acknowledge him. So we would sit there for a while until we were restless again and wanted to run about some more, or spy on the old woman living in that big house. I tried talking my sister into knocking on the front door of that pillared dwelling. But she would never go for it because it was my idea, and she would only agree to stand guard or go for help if I got hurt. I didn't like that compromise because it meant helping me after I got hurt. That didn't seem fair. I just wanted to see inside the house, to discover how close it resembled my imagination. I thought of that woman as part of the past, that she looked dead to me. I also wanted to picture her going to London or buying Milk Duds and seeing a movie, or disco dancing to Saturday Night Fever. I didn't think she had any friends, and without friends it's hard to have fun. I didn't have any friends either except my sister—she was my friend. But she was younger than me, and I still couldn't convince her to do the things that I wanted her to do. She even got it into her head that she could make me do certain things, and soften my spirit to her will.

I had tried very hard with my imagination to picture the furniture, or the rooms, maybe one of them had a canopy bed like mine, but bigger and better, not the cheap version that my parents bought at Sears with the matching dresser and mirror. I wanted to know what kind of clothes the woman wore who lived in that house and if she was a refined lady. I imagined her having a posh accent. I didn't want her to hear my American twang, so crude, a ruffian with stringy hair and eyes that were too big and brown. A round face. I didn't know whether I was supposed to like my face or not, but I did know that I sounded different from everyone else, and I looked different. My sister blended in more, even with that awkward way she ran. She was only four or five, and when a kid is that young, adults cannot be too harsh. Whenever she did something wrong or got caught, everyone felt sorry for her, like the time she stole a whole roll of Starburst and my mother made her return it to the store. The owner ended up giving her a lollipop after my sister burst into tears, embarrassed. My mother, however, was firm, trying to teach her a lesson. I ended up with nothing for being good, and she got candy. So I figured it wouldn't be any different with these folks at the abbey, a couple cannibals eating children for dinner, the reason I was afraid to knock on their door. I thought they might have dead bodies in the basement and maybe that's why there were so many ghosts creeping about the abbey. But eventually I came to find out that there was no old lady, there were no bodies, and the Hondas and Toyotas parked outside belonged to young men, parishioners, studying to be vicars. I was so disappointed. No wonder

Henry VIII tossed up the whole thing and figuratively said, to hell with the church. Maybe the old lady moved into the same nursing home as my great-grandmother. But that was somewhere in Torrance, California, and we were in Thetford England where no one even knew what a "Torrance" was, let alone the face and frail body of my poor grandmother who I decided to outlive—not only making it to 99 years old, but maybe even 101. That seemed like a good age because I could eat ice cream whenever I wanted and stay up late on Saturday nights watching the horror flicks. But I guess I knew for sure that those movies weren't really scary because I had already met ghosts, and they were just lonesome and wanted to play like us kids.

SUMMER

SPECULATIVE FICTION

Belko's Ogre-Extermination Service

P.G. Badzey

"Remind me again, Marcus," said Miranda with a sidelong glance. "Why are we sneaking up to the back door of this place? I thought Tovar and his cousin were on good terms."

I nodded, watching the stocky figure of our dwarven friend Tovar as he gently knocked on the door of the squat stone building. He looked back at us, the evening light casting shadows on his bearded face, making him look a bit sinister.

"They are on good terms. Rofor said to be discreet. We're being discreet."

Miranda lifted a lock of golden hair over the point of her ear, looking unconvinced. "Tovar and Rofor are dwarves. Dwarves are hardly discreet. I don't see why we couldn't just meet Rofor in the tavern. It's warmer."

I considered pointing out that we, as mercenaries, didn't always get to choose the most comfortable locales for our activities. I then thought better of it. Miranda might take it as an invitation for a debate and we didn't have time for that.

The door to the building opened a crack, releasing a shaft of golden light that brightened the dimness of this autumn evening. I saw another person backlit in the opening, speaking to Tovar. Our friend nodded and motioned to us.

A small figure emerged from the shadows, only half my size. Shamlin, our resident halfling and procurer of all things monetary, smiled up at me.

"I hope he has beer," he said. He followed Miranda and me as we slipped across the street. "And chicken. A little cheese would be nice."

I made a mental note to get to the table fast. Although Shamlin's head barely reached my sternum, we might get only crumbs if we let him get started before us.

A rule to live by: get to the food before the halfling.

I paused at the door as the others entered, ushered in by Tovar. I put a hand on his shoulder.

"Should I bring in Devany?" I asked. "I know dwarves usually don't like to have hill sprites around. And you said Rofor doesn't trust humans much, so I'm not sure I should go in either. Maybe she and I should just wait outside."

Tovar grunted and eyed me. He stood only as tall as my shoulder and his burly, stocky frame matched the shape of his cousin's house. "Rofor will behave himself, or he'll answer to me. Devany shouldn't wait outside in the cold and neither should you."

I turned away from the house and waved into the gloom. Soon, a foot-tall, naked woman with dragonfly wings whirred in and landed on my shoulder. She carried only a tiny sword and dagger, one strapped to each thigh.

"You're sure?" Devany asked, her cornflower-blue eyes uncertain as she gave the house a once-over.

"You'll be fine. Rofor has a reputation for an acid tongue, but Tovar will keep him in line."

"I have an odd feeling about this assignment," Devany whispered as we entered. "I mean, mysterious thefts at the dwarven mines and someone with an Ogre-Extermination Service? Very odd."

"I hear you. We won't do anything until tomorrow morning at any rate. We'll just have to watch out," I replied.

***

"I told you to watch out," Miranda said with a look of disapproval. "That ogre almost skewered you."

I grinned at her over the corpse of the ogre. "I did watch out. See? I'm still alive."

Miranda shook her head with a sigh. "Men." She lifted one foot onto a nearby rock and adjusted her bootstraps.

"A bit noisy for my taste," Shamlin said in a mild tone as he wiped his daggers in another dead ogre's purple hair. Slightly more than three and a half feet tall and plump, Shamlin looked like an inoffensive farmer— which was why his enemies rarely noticed him or his blades until too late.

I surveyed the forest around us. Our skirmish with the ogres concluded, it returned to a peaceful silence, broken now by an occasional bird song.

"Any dwarf knows there's nothing wrong with the clash of arms," replied Tovar, "but then again, you're not a dwarf." He wiped off his double-bladed axe and stumped over to jerk his spear out of the chest of a third ogre.

Shamlin shrugged. "Yes, but we're supposed to be following your cousin's trail. It doesn't help to alert the ogres we're hunting. And why did Rofor take off before we got up this morning?"

Tovar looked thoughtful, stroking his beard. "He might have suddenly realized something about the ogre attacks and left to find out. He's not exactly the wisest of my cousins."

Miranda glided over to my side, wrinkling her delicate nose in distaste and giving me a look with her amazing violet eyes.

"In that we agree," she said. "It's almost like he didn't trust us. What was so important that he couldn't wait? Not that I want to be in earshot of him, mind you."

"Maybe he had second thoughts after the little dust-up about Devany," I replied. "Or maybe he doesn't trust us since we're not all dwarves. Or maybe he wasn't sure about hiring Belko's Ogre-Extermination Service in the first place. Or..."

Shooting a look at Tovar, I wisely withheld any further opinions of his cousin. Rofor's description of the ogres and their parentage lingered in my head, as did his disdainful and crude comments about Devany when we were introduced last night. Much to my surprise and pleasure, Tovar lost no time in giving Rofor an earful about respect, something that later drew a shy expression of thanks from Devany. It was a good thing Tovar stepped in, or I would have.

"I don't like this," Miranda whispered. "Something's not right."

I had my own suspicions, but after being around her long enough, I learned to appreciate Miranda's sense for intrigue. She had seen enough skullduggery in the Imperial Court to make her wary. If she sensed something, I would be wise to pay attention.

Still, from what Tovar said, it seemed that Belko had a good reputation. Every dwarf in this region of the Empire who paid handsomely for his services saw ogre attacks decrease. The bleached ogre skulls that Belko produced as evidence of his prowess certainly seemed authentic. However, I wasn't sure how one dwarf, no matter how capable, could take down ogres that easily by himself. He should probably be a king's champion making a much better living if he were that good.

I shrugged. "Let's just keep our eyes open. Everyone ready?"

"Ready as I'll ever be," sang out a cheery voice.

Devany landed on my shoulder and sat, leaning back on her hands. If it weren't for the wings, small size, and lack of clothes, she looked like a miniature elf: slender, pretty and graceful, with golden hair, like Miranda.

Fortunately, to keep the eyes of the male population in their heads, Miranda did wear clothes—expensive ones at that, even when battling

48

smelly ogres. Her indigo and violet travel dress fit every curve of her supple shape and the side slits gave a great view of toned legs and stylish little black boots. Her attire was completely unsuited to tracking evildoers in the wilderness, but, as she reminded me often, a countess had to keep up appearances. Despite all our adventures together, it still amazed me that her wardrobe never seemed to suffer.

"Come on," said Tovar, replacing his axe and taking up his spear. "It will be evening in a few hours. We'll have to make camp if we don't find Rofor soon. I just hope the ogres haven't captured him. He can be annoying and they might not keep him alive."

Annoying? If Rofor started in with his verbal abuse, the ogres were to be pitied. They might kill him just to save their hearing.

Shamlin and Devany ghosted ahead in the shadows to scout our path as we followed Tovar out of the ravine. He led us up to a ridge, then through a copse of trees. The afternoon sun cast a patchwork of shadows on the leaf-strewn ground under our boots. I smelled pines, alders, and then a campfire and meat of some kind cooking.

I hoped it wasn't Rofor. We needed the money.

Devany flew back at us, finger to her lips in warning, then zipped off to rejoin Shamlin. We followed her, much more slowly now, to a jumble of grey rocks near a clearing.

Miranda crouched down next to me, laying her hand on a moss-covered boulder as she peered ahead. "I thought so."

Rofor sat in front of a tree, trussed up like a chicken ready for the cook pot. Conveniently enough, a large cauldron steamed over a merry campfire in the center of the clearing. One ogre stood over it, stirring the contents and adding herbs of some kind. Another ogre peered into the vessel, licking his lips and occasionally prodding the cook with an elbow.

A particularly large ogre strode back and forth on the other side of the pot, muttering to himself. Clad in chainmail, he bore a sword and club at his belt. Occasionally he ran a hand through his dark blue hair and stopped, considering something, then shook his head and continued pacing.

Tovar nodded at him. "That's probably a sub-chieftain, from the looks of his gear. We'd need to take him out first. The other two might run if we do that."

I nodded as Shamlin joined us. Devany landed on my shoulder again.

"Tovar and Shamlin can take on the chief," I said, scratching lines in the dirt. "Miranda can provide fire support from here. Devany and I will keep the other two busy. After that, we'll cut Rofor from his ropes and—"

A bellow from the clearing interrupted me and we peeked over the rocks.

A red-bearded dwarf stomped into the clearing, carrying a war hammer on his shoulder and looking murderous.

"What in Hades are you doing?"

The ogre chief jumped in surprise and took a step back.

Tovar smiled at me. "That's Belko. This should be fun. We can just watch the show."

Expecting Belko to take care of the ogres, I relaxed, but a sense of alarm started to build when the other ogres didn't draw weapons. Instead, they joined their leader, looking chagrined.

The ogre chief spread his hands. "We find this one sneaking near hideout. He close to finding star-metal. He say he know you and we be sorry. We not believe but he show us paper with your name on it, so we hold him for you. Not want to eat boss' friend."

"I knew it!" Miranda hissed.

Belko glared at the ogre chief. "He has the paper, you idiot, because that was our contract. He wasn't supposed to find you. I was. We were supposed to go through with the fake battle, then I'd come back with news that I'd driven you off. He pays me. Then I meet you oafs in the forest and we split it, like usual. How did he get here?"

The chieftain scratched his head. "That what I try to figure out."

"Ha!" shouted Rofor. "It was easy for anyone with brains! I started thinking about this real hard last night. I located all the ogre attacks on the map, then figured out a likely spot equidistant from all of them. My mistake was not bringing my cousin and his friends. They'd make short work of you, you addle-pated, stew-brained, weasel-faced son of a goat!"

Oh boy. And he's just getting warmed up.

Belko roared with laughter. "As if I'd be scared of a few dwarves! Any of your relatives will be easy pickings."

Rofor smirked. "Ever hear of the Five Aces? I can see from your pale expression that you have, you goblin turd. They're on their way and they'll carve up your bony buttocks and roast them, along with your squinty eyes for dessert."

"Eww…" said Devany, looking a bit green.

Belko spun around to the ogre leader, frowning. "If the Aces are on their way, we have to get out of here, you lummox. Get those other two idiots on the move. I want all the star-steel out of here and on the hunter's path in five minutes."

He turned back to Rofor, a wicked gleam in his eye, hefting his hammer. "But for you, you inadequate sack of demon spit, I'm going to flatten your pointed head."

"Coward," muttered Tovar from next to me, gripping his weapons.

"Without your mother to help you, I doubt if you have the guts!" shouted Rofor, red-faced. "You lily-livered, pox-faced, beetle-brained excuse for a devil-worshipper! You don't have the gumption to fight anyone who's not tied up!"

"You're going to wear this hammer head in your brain-pan!" Belko yelled back, advancing on his prisoner.

With that, Tovar charged, raising his spear to throw.

"Okay!" I said, hastily lifting my shield. "I guess we're on plan B now."

"What's plan B?" asked Miranda.

Tovar's spear thumped into the side of one of the ogres.

"Improvisation," I replied.

"As usual," retorted Shamlin as he raced off.

I charged out as Miranda clambered on top of a boulder. She unleashed a veritable storm of little darts of fire from her hands. The tiny magic balls peppered the ogres and Belko, detonating with sharp cracks and making them stagger. They cried out in pain and anger.

The chieftain turned on me first, as I had hoped, with Tovar charging Belko and one of the ogres. Devany turned invisible and I heard the whirring of her wings heading off towards Rofor. I focused on the matter at hand, which was a good thing because this particular ogre chief was ambidextrous. It took all my skill to block with my shield and dodge. As it was, I took a good shot in my right bracer that almost made me lose my weapon. A shadow of movement darted behind the chief and I crouched, shield raised.

I dropped my mace and raised my hand, casting a ball of magical light on the chief's nose. He bellowed and stepped back, blinking, right into Shamlin's twin blades. He stumbled and took a swipe at the halfling, who rolled out of the way and darted back in. I called my mace and it glowed, vibrated, then sprang to my hand. I stepped in with a good thump on the chieftain's right leg that cracked bone. The chief's leg buckled, but he managed to swing his club around. I barely got my shield up in time and fell backwards from the blow, rolling into a crouch, shield up.

The chief slashed at Shamlin with his sword. Shamlin leaped over the blade. The ogre caught him with a backhand club stroke and Shamlin flew through the air, sprawling into a bush.

I charged in, aiming for the ogre's sword-hand. I broke his forearm, then his other shoulder, then his head.

Not waiting for anything else, I turned my attention to Shamlin.

He gasped in pain. "Ribs."

I put a hand to Shamlin's side, whispering a prayer to Saint Raphael, the Healer Angel. Warm energy surged through me into his wound. With my inner, spiritual vision, I saw his bones knit back together, his blood vessels heal and inflammation subside.

I looked up at the battle in the glade. Tovar and one of the ogre guards exchanged hearty blows, the dwarf's axe blade ringing as it met the ogre's sword. The other ogre lurched through a steady stream of Miranda's fire and ice darts with an upraised axe, heading towards her perch on the boulder.

Devany had done her work well. Rofor was free of his bonds and Belko had lost his hammer. The two dwarves slugged away at each other with fists and boots, shouting insults in a mashed garble of Dwarven, Human, and, inexplicably, Elven.

Tovar dropped his opponent with an axe strike to the chest, then turned to help Miranda.

The last ogre swung at Miranda, who leaped over the weapon—a neat trick in that dress. Devany winked into view on the ogre's shoulder, stabbing at its head, but it dodged and swatted at her with a meaty hand. She spun out of the way. This gave Miranda the opening to send a screaming bullet of acid into the ogre's heart.

Meanwhile, the fight between Rofor and Belko transformed into a roiling, dusty wrestling match, complete with biting and clawing. The pair tripped, fell and rolled into the copse of trees and off the edge of the nearby slope. We heard them bounce down the hillside with audible thumps.

"Ooh," said Devany, wincing as she flew over. "That one's going to hurt in the morning. And that one, and—ouchie! Gonna need some of your healing magic, Marcus."

The others joined us.

Tovar shot a glance down the slope and shrugged. "Rofor always had a temper, particularly when he felt he was getting cheated. He has a very visceral reaction to betrayal."

"I'll say," noted Shamlin.

The shouting and thumping down the hillside receded into the distance, then fell silent.

"Yep," said Devany, landing on my shoulder. "That did it. They knocked each other out."

"Good," said Miranda, brushing dust from her dress with a sniff. "I can't say I approved of their language. And their Elven grammar was atrocious."

"What do we do next?" Shamlin asked. "I heard them talking about star-metal."

Tovar nodded. "If that's what the metalsmiths in this region were producing, no wonder Belko was trying to cheat everyone. Star-steel is lighter than regular steel and twice as strong, so it makes great armor. It's worth a lot."

"So, the metalsmiths will pay a good fee to get their wares back?" Shamlin mused.

Tovar nodded and Shamlin looked pleased.

"What do we do about them?" asked Devany, pointing down the slope.

"Tie up Belko," I said, "so we can get him to the town guard. And gag him."

Miranda raised an eyebrow at me. "What about Rofor?"

I had sudden visions of trundling back to town with Belko, a cartload of star-metal and an injured, angry Rofor in tow—with a fully functional mouth. It made my ears hurt already.

I looked at Tovar. He shrugged.

"On second thought," I said, "better gag both of them."

Chase

Terry Black

I gritted my teeth, said "Here goes nothing!" and turned the ignition. The engine sputtered and caught, the air shimmered and sparkled like diamonds, and my 2013 Saturn SL launched itself backward in time. I felt a thrill of exhilaration, knowing my quantum-based adjustments to the car's engine were functioning just as designed.

I goosed the accelerator, watching the years roll back on the digital Time-O-Meter, while the improvised LED labeled "Geographic Location" displayed one word: Antietam.

1864, 1863, 1862…I hit the brake, and my rust-colored Saturn came to a stop near one of the earliest battles of the American Civil War, on the banks of Antietam Creek. I hoped the cloak field would keep anyone from noticing a modern-day sedan, parked improbably under a stand of cottonwoods.

Explosions shook the field. Cannon fire raised great clouds of choking smoke, like toxic fog. I heard hoarse cries, scattered gunshots, and saw infantrymen scrambling like ants over the facing hillside—into the terrible reality of war.

Something bleeped on the dashboard. The proximity alert. Someone was approaching—but not through space. I was being followed through time.

Impossible, I thought, but there it was—a dark red blip against the backdrop of centuries, drawing steadily closer. I punched the accelerator, and fled into the past.

Next stop was the Mayflower Landing—a spectacular sight, as the grand old triple-masted cargo ship entered a lush harbor, where the New

World lay beckoning to a ship full of Pilgrims. Their influence on the developing colonies would be seminal and historic, but I had no time to reflect on that because the proximity alert was bleeping louder now.

I fled again, to the Magna Carta signing, which established the precedent for the modern rule of law. The Norman Conquest, bloody and pivotal, enshrining 1066 as the year that changed history. The birth of Jesus, in a manger outside Bethlehem, under the glow of a wayward star. The construction of the Great Pyramid of Giza, an engineering marvel, built on the backs of a thousand slaves. Still my relentless pursuer kept coming.

Finally, in a Paleolithic rainforest long before the first protohumans emerged onto the African savannah, I stopped and waited for my time-travelling shadow. *This ends now*, I thought, determined to stand my ground.

There was a jolt, a crackle, the stench of ozone. White light blossomed in front of me. And there, just a few feet away, was the temporal vehicle that had chased me through all of human history, and beyond.

A Volkswagen Jetta.

"Sorry to bother you honey," said my wife, jumping out with a brown paper bag, "but you forgot your lunch. I took the other car, hope you don't mind."

Gravel Road Gratitude

Lisa Congdon

The sound of gravel crunching under his worn work boots was the only noise that greeted Hugh's ears as he trudged along. Lungs burnin' and lips tinglin' from the bitter wind, he cursed that damn rabbit-chasin' dog. He'd crossed a few fields and climbed through more than one fence before he'd realized a mite too late that he should have just left the mutt to fend for himself against any critters bigger'n him that might be roamin' as night approached.

Flippin' up the collar on his coat to shield his ears, Hugh thought about his warm home and waitin' wife. She'd be worryin' herself at the window by now. It weren't like her hard-workin' husband to not come round when she called out suppertime, and by the slant of the sun behind the trees, he knew he'd missed that by a sight.

He halted his pace to catch his breath and determine his bearings while watchin' the orange and pink hues color the sky behind the eighty foot evergreens that dotted the landscape. Relief flooded his face as he caught sight of chimney smoke over the next rise. Or, at least he was fairly certain it was chimney smoke.

"Could be ole Politan's place, I reckon. Or more'n likely the Agelit Farm, if I was a bettin' man." Old Neo Politan was as curmudgeonly as a bull in spring and would look none too kindly on someone showing up on his doorstep unannounced. He'd fuss a bit, but Hugh knew he'd eventually give in to offerin' a ride. Fin Agelit was a tall Irish fella with youth on his side and plenty of neighborly leanin's. He'd be happy as a lark to give Hugh a lift. "I sure do hope that's the Farm, I do. No matter. At this point they'll both git me where I'm aimin' to be."

He struck out again with a renewed sense of direction and a bit more hope than he'd had minutes before. It would take a few more miles of aching joints, but he'd be home again in no time with sweet Tammy Lynn fussin' over him, to be sure. He blew on his fingers to bring some warmth, knowin' it was futile what with the temperature likely droppin' near thirty by now. Neo had told him that very mornin' over an early breakfast at Meg's Diner that autumn would be short as a corn stalk and winter would come round right quick. Looks like he was right on the money since the leaves had barely started to turn and they already littered the ground around his feet.

Hugh settled deeper into his faded work jacket and set out toward what he hoped was Fin's farm. Truth be told, he'd prefer Mrs. Politan's mince meat pie to warm his belly, but Neo had said she was ailin' a bit so he wouldn't want to put her out at all. Besides, Fin's place was closer to home and Hugh wasn't a man to want to keep his worryin' wife waitin' too long for him to return.

As his feet scuffed over the dusty gravel road, his knees were fixin' to complain about his impromptu hike across the county. He didn't fancy the sheriff out lookin' for him, at Tammy Lynn's insistence, only to find his weary bones at the side of the road in the wee hours of the morn', a coyote or two for company. "Nope. Best to keep movin' and pay no attention to old bones so's I can get where I'm goin'."

With thoughts tumblin' about like the brittle leaves, he continued on resolutely, reminiscin' about his life and the many gravel roads he'd travelled on his way to sixty-four. Back in seventy-three, soon after Hugh had returned home from his brief stint in the Army, he'd set his sights on workin' with his daddy on the family's cattle ranch.

Hugh smiled broadly to himself, rememberin' fondly the spit and vinegar that eagerly accompanied his twenty-second year of life. The young ladies down at Smokey Jim's Tavern fancied a fella in uniform, freshly returned home from lands unknown. If a man could hold his liquor and didn't get mixed up in too many fights, they'd sure as anything be lined up for a spin around the dance floor. Hugh had willingly obliged on many an occasion and even managed to steal a kiss or two out in the back of the hay barn on those hot summer nights.

Hugh snapped a wheat shaft off as he walked and stuck it between his chapped lips to keep his body as occupied as his mind. Memory lane had him thinkin' about how he'd barely had time to roll down the windows on his pickup truck and split gravel and a few beers with his buddies that year before his life took its first big turn.

One humid, sticky August night after an even hotter day of balin' hay, Hugh and the boys found themselves sneakin' off down the gravel road to town and throwin' back a few cold ones at the tavern. Tammy Lynn swept up to the table as she usually did, swappin' empty pitchers of beer with full ones and collectin' dinner remains as she went. This night in particular, she smacked the back of Hugh's head with a rolled up towel and told him to get his filthy work boots off her clean table. Up till then, she hadn't said more'n ten words to him in as long as he could remember.

Her strawberry blonde hair was tucked behind her ears, cheeks flushed from hours of deliverin' southern fried chicken dinners to the locals come in from the summer heat. Her blue eyes were so clear like the swimmin' hole down by the waterfalls, and Hugh realized he could swim in their depths forever. He'd never seen anyone so beautiful or alive. Her fiery temper had been witnessed by most town folks at one time or another and he was no exception. A smarter man would have dropped his feet along with his smile and steered clear. "I never was none too smart, then or now, I reckon." He chuckled out loud at what had come next.

The first thing he did was stand up real slow, remove his hat and set it on the dusty table. Then he winked at his buddies, relieved Tammy Lynn of her serving tray and towel, and quickly drew her toward the dance floor. She hadn't protested all that much, and he liked to think it was because she secretly liked him all along, not because it was the last thing she had expected, him having caught her off guard and all. He had twirled her around the floor, the country twang emanating from the jukebox pulling them closer with every beat. He knew by the third song that she'd be his wife some day. That trip down a dusty gravel road from his daddy's farm to the bar at the edge of town had certainly changed his life.

Tammy Lynn and Hugh dated steady for a few months, and his plan was to save up enough money to buy a pretty little ring and be on one knee by Christmas Eve. He'd then buy them a small house with a picket fence once they were married, and he'd work his daddy's farm till some day it became theirs. It was a good plan, and with a beautiful, spirited woman like Tammy Lynn by his side, Hugh couldn't have been a happier man.

It had all worked out in the end, and as Hugh walked along the lonely gravel road now, cold hands stuffed into his blue jeans pockets, feet more tired than they had a right to be, he smiled the weathered smile of a man who knew he was loved well by a good woman for many a year. He'd been blessed with a life that many others weren't fortunate enough to have, with a few broken fences and a couple scars to give it character.

Kicking at a stone in the road and sending it flyin' into the ditch, Hugh thought about how one of those scars had left its mark much earlier in his youth than he would have ever imagined.

While Hugh had been off learnin' to be a soldier, he hadn't known that the farm was sufferin' as silently as his daddy had been, much longer than his daddy's pride would ever let on. Several summer droughts and a particularly bad twister had torn up the land, diverted the creek that had run through their property, and destroyed the outbuildings that housed their livestock. All the while, the cancer had ravaged his daddy's body, bendin' his frame and loosenin' his hold on his livelihood and the family inheritance. Hugh knew he should have seen the signs when he returned from servin' his country. However, he'd still been a boy in a man's body, in denial and not yet ready to see what was laid out before him.

Before the last of the deep snows covered the ground that winter when Hugh was twenty two, Hugh had travelled all the way to the end of the gravel road on the other side of town, and laid his daddy's body to rest, right next to his late mama's. Hugh had grieved for the mother he'd lost when he was a small boy, and the father he hadn't been fortunate enough to know yet as a man.

By the time the daffodils peeked their cautious heads above the frozen ground, he'd had to sell off the remaining cattle to pay the hospital debts, and eventually sell the farm itself when he couldn't make it turn a profit any longer.

That first year without his family threatened to turn Hugh's anger inward and keep it bottled up. But his lovely Tammy Lynn slowly turned his anger to dust and his thoughts to their future. Together they built a whole new life. All in all, he reckoned, they'd raised two great children who loved the Lord and their parents and who had gone off to find their own lives and happiness. He'd call that a blessed life.

A hoot owl interrupted Hugh's musin' and he realized that as his boots crunched along, night had surely fallen, dark and silky and cold. Fortunately, the late summer rains had driven gullies into the side of the road, making a moonlit path that would lead him to his neighbor's place. It would be none too soon for his likin'.

Hugh figured that mangy farm dog he'd been chasin' had long since returned home, with or without the rabbit he'd taken off after. If Hugh had seen fit to let that rascal do his huntin' on his own, they'd both be tucked inside tonight near the fireplace with full bellies and warm feet.

Sighin', he picked up his pace, as much for warmth as to be finished with this walk down memory lane. He worried about his Tammy Lynn. Surely she'd be frettin' and callin' the neighbors to see where Hugh had gotten himself off to. It wasn't uncommon for him to be found helpin' a fellow farmer with a breeched calf or a late harvest. Now that it was truly dark and well past supper time, with no word about Hugh's whereabouts, Tammy Lynn would be callin' out the search party.

Hugh took stock of his progress and realized that a house with yellow porch lights beckoned him from about a half mile or so away. He didn't quite recognize the lay of the land in the dark by foot, but he knew with every step he wasn't so far from home now. Neighbors in these parts were as close as kin. He walked on, encouraged and ignorin' his aching joints. Before long, a howl and a yip greeted his steps as he approached the old wooden front porch of his long-time friend Neo. He took the first step slowly, holding onto the railin' as he lifted his foot for the next, happy to feel somethin' other than gravel under his soles.

"Hey there, Hugh. Whatcha doing out here in the middle of the night? Nearly scared me half to death walkin' up on me like that." Neo sat on a porch swing, and the squeak, squeak, squeak attested to years with no oil applied. It was comfortin' and Hugh was glad for it.

"Just takin' a walk. Never know what a man might discover with a bit of fresh air and some time. Never know where a road might lead a man." Hugh reached the swing and plopped his weary body onto it with a satisfied grunt. Neo handed him his still warm mug of coffee and Hugh gulped it down gratefully.

"Well ain't that the truth, my friend. Never did a body no harm to get a little lost and find what he didn't even know he was missin'."

Hugh slid his glance over to the friend he'd known since before his mama passed on. Neo and he went way back, back to when they'd get teased in grammar school by the other kids about their names…Hugh Jeffort and Neo Politan. They guessed that's one of things that made them fast friends and kept them that way all these years. Neo was a man who kept his mouth closed unless he felt the need to share some wisdom or defend his property. He'd done a fine job of that tonight, and Hugh felt his good fortune swayin' on the swing beside him.

"Spose my Tammy Lynn will likely be wanting to see me home soon."

"Spose she will." The swing moved a bit more, then in unspoken unison each man made his way to Neo's old pickup and climbed in. For the next few minutes, neither spoke as the truck clambered over the gravel road that led them from Neo's place to Hugh's home.

"You know, a man can live a lifetime in the country and still find himself unexpectedly on a gravel road."

Neo nodded. He knew Hugh's story well and the roads he'd travelled.

"I found my wife at the end of a gravel road. I said goodbye to my daddy at the end of another. I've found heartache and love, all on different gravel roads between here and there. Tonight, these weary bones found memories as thick as molasses on a cold day in December. I found a peaceful heart for a life well lived. A less fortunate man might've missed the journey while tryin' to get to where he thought he was goin'."

Neo nodded once more. "A friend at the end of a gravel road can put a little pep back in an old man's step and have him seein' things that tired eyes could otherwise miss."

It was Hugh's turn to nod. He agreed completely. "Glad to be on the journey with you, my friend."

"And I, you." Neo pulled the truck up to the front porch of Hugh's old farmhouse as Tammy Lynn came out, screen door bangin' behind her. It was good to be home.

Hugh made his way up to Tammy Lynn at the top of the steps and the two of them put their arms around each other, grateful to have each other once more at the end of the long gravel road. They turned and Hugh held the door for his lovely Tammy Lynn and his wayward dog as they entered their home.

Gravel road gratitude is a fine thing indeed.

The Last Ferry

Jim Topping

They ran. Hand in hand they ran. Their feet splashed in puddles, soaking their shoes and pant legs.

"Do you think we'll make it?" she asked, breathlessly.

"I think so," he answered. "Keep running!"

They rounded the corner and the ticket booth came into view. He was relieved when he saw that a few cars were still driving up the ramp.

"They're still boarding," she said, hope in her voice.

They slid to a stop in front of the ticket booth. Thick glass mirrored their tense faces.

"Are we too late?" he asked, between heaving breaths.

"Looks like you just made it," the woman behind the glass smiled. "Two adults?"

"Yes, please," he said, pulling out his wallet and opening it.

"I have no money," he said, with shock in his voice. He looked hopefully at his date.

"How about you Jacqueline?"

She was already opening her purse. "We need twelve right? Six for each?"

"Yeah. If you don't have it, it's a long cold swim back to Bremerton," he said, worry in his voice.

She pulled some bills out of her purse. "Here you go," she said to the cashier as she slid them through the slot.

The woman traded the bills for two ferry tickets and said, "You better hurry. They're close to casting off."

Grabbing the tickets in one hand and Terry's hand in the other, Jacqueline shouted, "Come on, we can make it! Even if it means a leap in the dark onto the deck, we can make it!"

The wind of their passage roared in Terry's ears as they ran. Their footsteps echoed inside the pedestrian walkway. No one else was there. If they made it, they would be the last ones aboard.

As they ran, Terry thought about the day. It was their second date. Take the ferry across to Seattle and wander the city all day. They'd had a blast and he really enjoyed her company. They were having so much fun that during dinner they had lost track of time. If they missed this last ferry, he wasn't sure what they would do.

They rounded the last bend and saw a guard standing by the gate that was still ajar. Were they too late?

"Hurry along folks, we're all set to leave," the guard said as they approached.

Heaving a huge sigh of relief, they careened past him, down the ramp and onto the deck.

"Wow, we made it!" she said laughing.

"Yeah, we did!" he exclaimed, joining in her laughter.

The ferry cast off and the deck trembled slightly as the vessel moved out into Elliott Bay, the picturesque skyline of the city reflecting in her smiling eyes.

They reached for each other, and as the breeze tousled their hair, their lips met with their first kiss.

Reptile Rhapsody

Terry Black

I should have let well enough alone.

I mean, was it worth a road trip back to Snakeskin, Arizona in the hottest part of the hottest summer on record, just to pry up the floorboards of my old bedroom—and get back the comic book I left there years ago, when we moved out?

The comic book was *The Amazing Spider-Man #7*, the first appearance of the Lizard, a herpetologist named Curt Connors who injects himself with reptile venom and becomes a scaly monster. It creeped me out big time. It didn't help that the neighborhood was crawling with lizards that used to gape at me with their black spotlight eyes and tongue-flick whenever I'd go by, flick-flick, flick-flick, like some sort of cold-blooded Morse code.

It took seven hours to drive to Snakeskin Gulch. Somewhere along the way, between Dead Man's Ridge and Heatstroke Hollow, my radiator warning light came on. By the time I pulled up in front of that old dustbowl ramshackle house on Bent Cactus Lane, I wasn't sure the car would be drivable afterward.

I went in. The door wasn't locked, the house long abandoned. The old wooden stair creaked as I made my way up to the second floor. I crept into my old bedroom, backlit by the sun through a filmy, broken-out window, and found the floorboard with my comic book under it. Just as I reached for it, a lizard scampered in front of me.

The herpetologist in *Spider-Man #7* loses his arm. Because of the lizard venom, it grows back. I thought how lucky he was to be whole again, how turning into a rough-scaled monster was a small price to pay to get back a part of yourself that seemed lost forever.

Not an arm, necessarily. It doesn't have to be a body-part; it could be a part of your spirit, a wellspring of courage, a mad rejuvenation of the life-force that keeps you charging ahead into the next tomorrow. The future beckons: get ready to embrace it. That was the message of *Spider-Man #7*.

Suddenly I knew that I didn't need my comic book. I already knew what I had to do to make myself complete.

I plucked the lizard off the floor, stuffed it into my mouth and gulped it down.

Root Beer

Thom Kerr

I

It was her favorite drink until the accident. It was a Tuesday about three or four weeks ago. She was driving east on the boulevard. The day was clear and warm, not a cloud in the sky. Traffic was almost non-existent. A beige Buick station wagon was moving west on the other side of the divider. A delivery truck was about half a block in front of her. There had been quite a few cars parked along the curb back by the high school where people were enjoying the tennis courts and running track. The baseball field is on the other side of the school and there were probably people there too, but she couldn't see them when she drove by.

The truck in front of her had the back open and she could see some barrels and canisters loaded inside. There was a bit of bluish smoke coming from the tailpipe of the Buick. "Probably burning a little oil" she thought to herself as she passed the fire station.

Looking ahead, she saw the delivery truck pulling away from the stop sign at Main Street and head into the dip on the other side. She did not see the strap come loose; perhaps it had been loose all along. Maybe the loader had carelessly not even fixed the strap, but as the truck began to climb out of the dip, she definitely saw the barrels and canisters slide to the back and fall onto the boulevard in front of her. She heard the noise as they clattered to the asphalt and split open. She could smell the sweet aroma of the liquid pooled into the dip just in front of where she stopped behind the mess.

The truck driver had also heard the crash and pulled quickly to the side of the boulevard to assess the situation. Five hundred gallons of root beer syrup lay pooled at the bottom of the dip.

Time passed, police came, streets were closed and traffic diverted. Decisions were made and the Fire Department was called to clean up the mess. They were just down the street after all.

High pressure hoses directed a stream of water on the mess, and the root beer foamed up, and foamed up more, and foamed up more. The ensuing tsunami of foam engulfed her car, still parked behind the dip and filled the windows.

II

Months later life had almost gotten back to normal, sans root beer. Her insurance company had made arrangements to clean the car although occasionally the faint, sweet smell of sarsaparilla would waft from the air conditioning vent.

She suffered through all the jokes and teasing that she had anticipated. Most of it came from her sister Cindy. Most had been good natured, coming from friends and family. Occasionally an anonymous can of Barqs would appear in the mail box.

Last night she had loaned the sedan to Cindy. PTA meetings waited for no man or woman and Cindy's car was in the shop. About noon, she heard her car pulling into the drive and knew Cindy was here.

Glancing out the front window she froze. This time Cindy had gone too far. From all appearances Cindy had gotten her car painted. The candy apple red was now a red umber metal flake. It looked just like root beer.

The front door flew open and Cindy burst in, beaming and laughing so hard that tears were running from her eyes. "Do you love it?" she asked. "Doesn't it make you thirsty just to look at it?" Cindy kept talking but most of what she said was not registering. A closer inspection was warranted.

It was a wonderful paint job. Very well done. Good quality paint. This seemed like the ultimate practical joke.

"Cindy," she said, "don't you have anything else to spend your money on? Let's go for a drive!"

They got in the car and headed east on the boulevard, past the fire station, through the dip in the road, where she still fancied that she could hear the rubber of the tires sticking just a bit more to the asphalt than they had a block back.

Wheeling into the strip mall, she guided the freshly painted vehicle into a parking spot in front of the market. "Wait here Cindy," she ordered her sister and ran into the store.

When she returned, she placed a bag in the back seat, slid behind the wheel and started the car. Back on the boulevard she continued east, ignoring the flourish of questions about "What's in the bag?" from her sister.

III

"What bag?" she asked back.

"The bag from the market." Cindy said.

"I don't know what you're talking about."

They drove for about an hour into the countryside. Cindy had given up trying to learn more about their destination or the bag. They rode in silence for most of that time. Smooth jazz emanated softly from the door speakers of the root beer car, and it was a pleasant day. The silence between the two was not awkward or pensive. It was natural. She and Cindy were sisters after all; often they could intuit what each other were thinking. Often they did not even bother to try.

That is the thing about siblings. Familiarity and love could replace a need to entertain or fill silence with blather.

Just about the time that Cindy was going to demand a pit stop, she pulled into a narrow lane that disappeared into the trees. She put the car in park and set the brake, got out and went to open the gate. Too late Cindy realized she had missed her chance to peek into the mystery bag.

They left the gate open and drove about a quarter of a mile further up the lane. As they crested a rise, there appeared a ramshackle old cabin with a couple of small outbuildings.

"What is this place?" asked Cindy, previous urges for a rest stop now completely given over to curiosity.

"This is Mr. Wilson's hunting cabin," she answered. "He doesn't hunt much anymore, and he loaned it to me for a few days. Hope you don't have any pressing appointments. Mom agreed to take care of the kids. You and I are going to spend two days in the country, no TV, no newspaper and no distractions beyond what is already here."

"What is already here?" Cindy asked.

"A forest, a stream, fresh air, sunshine and quiet," she replied. "What more do we need?"

"Maybe a root beer colored car and some ice cream" Cindy quipped. "We have the car, but if that was ice cream in the bag, it is undoubtedly liquid by now. We've been driving forever."

"Not ice cream, something better." She reached for the bag and smiled. "Come on, I'll show you the cabin." They went into the cabin that was a single room shack. The old room reminded her of one of those western-themed restaurants with all the old stuff nailed up on the walls.

IV

After a quick tour of the hunting cabin, Cindy looked in the fridge and grabbed a couple of root beers. Opening hers, she took a long draught and wiped the back of her sleeve across her mouth. She handed the other to her sister who politely declined. "Sorry Cindy, I still can't imagine drinking root beer ever again."

They sat at the table and Cindy said, "As excited as I am to spend the rest of the weekend with you, it is now time to show me what's in the bag sis." Cindy reached for the bag and peeked in the top. Her eyes widened and she turned the bag over, spilling the contents on the table, lots of green banknotes piled up. Mostly 20 dollar bills although she could see several 50's and quite a few 100's as well.

Also clattering onto the table was a large butcher knife. It looked brand new, not even scratched. Cindy looked her sister in the eye, "Tell me you didn't rob the grocery store" she admonished.

"I can't tell you that; I did rob the grocery store. Let's see how much money we got," she smiled. It didn't seem right to either of them that it would be so easy to rob a grocery. "The beauty of hitting a market is that you don't need to bring anything with you to succeed. The butcher knives are on the rack in the kitchenware department. You can just help yourself, and there are bags at every check stand. "I meant to get some cookies too. Must have forgotten them. I was so excited."

They counted almost 9,000 dollars on the table, most of it in small bills, easy to pass. The butcher knife went into Mr. Wilson's cutlery drawer. She looked at Cindy, "I haven't had that much fun in years" she said. "It reminded me of when we used to hit the photomat on 17th Street. Those guys never realized that all we had was a water pistol, and the thrill just got better each time. Sometimes I am amazed that we actually robbed the same photomat five times in two weeks. Let's stop at the grocery store again on our way home."

Round Three

Jim Topping

The announcer's voice blared out of the old TV speaker, "Rounnnd three!"

The two boxers advanced into the ring and the action began. The sparring and posturing reflected in Roy's still eyes. He sat, drowning in the arm chair, captivated by the black and white images projected from the screen. He was oblivious to the footsteps entering the room.

"Goddamnit Roy, I thought that boxing crap was over an hour ago."

Sharon's grating voice went unnoticed by Roy. His only movement was slow steady breathing. She moved over next to the TV. Bending to make her face even with the screen, she looked at Roy and shouted, "Hello! Is anybody home in there?"

Roy's eyes swiveled and bored into hers for three or four seconds, then rolled back to the boxing.

She stood up and regarded him with barely concealed hostility. Turning, she stomped from the room, storming down the hall to the bedroom.

This was it, her raging mind thought; the breaking point has been reached.

On the bed her suitcase waited. It was still open and awaiting the final articles to be placed inside. Roy's .44 Magnum was lying beside the suitcase. She gazed at its rusting frame.

"Everything in that bastard's life is rusting away, even me," she fumed at the empty room. After a few minutes of adrenalin fueled scurrying,

I'm all for workin' it.

I try not to make eye contact with anyone close to me for fear my hungry eyes might betray me. I have to be honest; I chose the bar over the café because I'm in need of a man, a man with strong hands who can hold his liquor…sort of. The "sort of" is key: I like 'em relaxed, but drunk men don't serve me well.

I slowly sway my shoulders to the beat of a seventies tune playing on the jukebox. Looking in his direction I smile slightly and whisper, "tequila…make it a double, salt and lime on the side."

I catch his wink and with a deep enticing voice I hear, "sure thing sweetie."

I hate that label, sweetie. But how does he know. I do look sweet and angelic from the neck up. But below, well that's a different story…I'm pure devil.

I smile and give him a wink of acknowledgement.

He sets the shot glass, salt shaker and lime wedge down on the bar in front of me.

"Enjoy doll."

Another word I hate…doll.

But I'm right, the cleavage pays off, or maybe it's the thigh high leather boots. With a sniff of the golden liquid I know it's the good stuff…really good. I throw it back, wet the back of my hand, pour on the salt, slowly lick it off then for a very long minute suck the lime dry. The noise of shattering glass hitting the floor turns all the heads in the bar towards the barkeep. Turning a slight shade of red from embarrassment, he picks his jaw up off the floor and kicks the broken shards off the floor mat beneath his feet. I notice his hands still shaking and the bulge that now appears between his thighs.

Yeah, I have that effect.

Another duo of shots spread out over the next couple of hours when he finally walks through the door. The longshoreman of my desire, tall, muscular, clean shaven and strong. I can tell by the way he shakes hands with some of the other men sitting at the bar that he has a strong grip. I like a strong grip. I catch his eye.

Yep, that's right, come my way.

The barkeep asks, "what'll it be buddy?"

He responds in a slow deliberate tone looking right at me.

"I'll have what she's having. And she'll have another."

I laugh again.

Silly man, he thinks he's in charge.

But I give him a nod of acknowledgement while I breathe in his scent. It is beyond my control and I want him.

Delivering the two double shots, I see the barkeep has lost the bulge that made him tempting. I raise my glass to mister man, who thinks he's in charge. He raises his glass and returns with a nod of his own along with a smile.

"Another round, Joe." He orders.

Joe, such a typical name for a seaside saloon barkeep.

He slams the next two shot glasses down before us, shakes his head and turns away.

Lost out again to a man with bigger hands.

Lift, nod, swallow, lick, suck, repeat. After three more rounds I turn on my stool and stand up, shift my shoulders just enough to create the right amount of enticing jiggle at eye level, brush my hand across his shoulder and lean in with a breathy whisper, "I'll be outside."

I'm out the door, and before I even open my umbrella, I hear the squeak of the door and wet footsteps behind me.

"Good, I hate to be kept waiting." I say without turning around.

"I'm sure you don't…and shouldn't," he responds.

I know whichever way I walk, he will follow…and he does. I lead him down the hill and across the street to the rocky beach along a secluded cliffside wall. The rain has turned to a sexy light mist making his shirt nearly invisible.

Hmm…whatta waste.

I lean against the cliff, the heels of my thigh high boots digging into the heavy wet sand, my back pressed against the hard rocks. His hands roam my body… and I let them. They are as strong as I had imagined and grip me in all the right places. The feel of his bulge against me tells me it's time.

I slip my left hand inside his waistband and down his moist skin until I feel his hardness. I let myself wrap around him until he moans. I squeeze gently…then tight. My right hand slides up his neck, entangling my fingers into his thick wet curls. I pull his head into the perfect tilt. My moist lips skim his neck and my tongue follows across the cool dampness of his skin. I squeeze tighter between his legs, open my mouth wide until I feel the toothy snap. I hesitate briefly listening for that heavy moan to tell me he's at just the perfect moment. I grip even tighter and bite through the clean-shaven layers of his flesh and suck…hard. His juice is the perfect blend of tequila, salt air and sweet blood. I don't want to stop, I can't. His body is convulsing against mine with both pleasure and pain.

With my thirst mostly satisfied I pull my bite out of him, untangle my fingers from his hair and my other hand away from his thighs. His pants are wet when he falls limp to ground and I can still see a bulge inside his pants. Still craving his salty sweetness, the thirst rises again from deep within me, and I know there is more blood to be had. In a lust frenzied craze, I drop down beside him ripping at his jeans and bite down for the last bit of bloodied nectar.

I take a deep breath as I pull away. Closing my eyes, I breathe in his scent, and with the back of my hand I wipe a lingering drop of blood off the side of my mouth...then lick it clean. One more sweet taste. I look down at his lifeless pale body, the tastiest in three hundred years. Oh, how I love the salty seaside morsels the coast offers. I stare at the masculine beauty of him... Pity, a keeper for sure if I could ever learn to control my hunger. This one was oh so satisfying. I continue to enjoy the sight of him, take a deep, deep breath and hear myself moan.

I walk away from the cliffside shore, up the hill through the pines. The rain and mist have stopped, the clouds are parting and the moonlight follows me into the woods. Once home and miles from the seaside hamlet, I sit beside the flames. Between the windblown pines I enjoy the sight of the village lights flickering in the distance. Smiling, I'm satisfied beyond my dreams, though I wish I could have kept him for just a little while. The taste of him still sits on my lips, and I lick them slowly savoring every lingering, sweet last bit of him.

Oh, how I wish I hadn't left him lifeless... The tastiest are always worth another round.

Stiletto Heels

Jim Topping

Times have been tough in this ol' city. When jobs start going away, and people are out on the street, the need for a private eye goes pretty far down the priority list. But there's always one thing that keeps the lights on in lean times like these. Cheaters. Yep, cheaters, husbands cheating on their wives, wives cheating on husbands. Some would say it's a dirty business, but it keeps food on my table.

It had been a long day. The summer heat and irregular hours were wearing on me. The still humidity of my office was pushing my eyelids down, and it was hard to focus. The photos of the woman were striking. She was a looker all right. Her old man couldn't keep her at home, and the photos proved it.

I could hear a cold cocktail calling. Closing the file, I stood up. Hat in place, I locked the door and went out to find some refreshments. Outside the dusk was a like a hot cloak settling over the city. I retraced a familiar route down the dirty broken side-walk toward the corner. "Ostrich Bar" was spelled out in garish neon above the door. The place reeked of stale cigarette smoke, spilled beer and sweat. But it was my second home. Clomping across the matted carpet I alighted onto my regular stool.

I settled into place, elbows on the worn oak bar, when my eyes spied her. Stunning she was, in a dangerous sort of way. Her eyes, blue like the sky, bored straight into mine. A shiver went down my spine, and I hoped she didn't notice. I couldn't take my eyes off her. Her blonde mane was pulled around the right side of her heart shaped face and draped down over her chest. Her ivory skin blended with her hair and made her bright red lipstick impossible to miss. Her pouty lips matched an equally crimson dress.

There were three empty stools on each side of her. There wasn't a guy in the place with the balls to go near her.

Ernie, the bartender, managed to interrupt my trance.

What'll it be Joe, the usual?"

"What's she havin'?" my head motioning toward the blonde.

Raising his eyebrows, Ernie said, "The lady's havin' a gin and tonic."

A curious rush of anxiety went through me.

"Fine, make it two."

Ernie shook his head slowly as he prepared the cocktails. I wasn't sure if it was in admiration or resignation.

He strolled over the other side of the L-shaped bar and placed the drink in front of her. I could see him speak, and once again, following the motion of his head, her blue eyes bored into mine. Part of me wanted to run, but more of me wanted to stay.

I broke her stare and busied myself stirring my drink with the straw. Taking a sip I saw her slide off the stool to her feet. She walked around the corner of the bar and headed toward me. She was packing some serious curves into a short dress that clung to her body like a second skin. She glided with a willowy grace on long shapely white legs and five inch stiletto heels that matched the rest of her ensemble.

My glass rattled a little when I set it back down. She stopped at the stool next to me.

"Is this seat taken?" she asked. Her voice was sultry and firm.

The bar around us got quiet. Even the jukebox was curiously muted. A quick glance around revealed staring faces.

"No, it's free," I said, struggling to keep my voice even. Perspiration prickled my armpits.

She slid up onto the stool. Her drink materialized in front of her. Ernie was quick to make himself scarce.

"Do you make a habit of buying strange women drinks?"

"No," I said meeting her eyes. I sounded like a square.

"Not a soul in this place would give me the time of day, but you actually bought me a drink. That must be quite a pair you're sportin'."

"Name is Joe," I said, extending my hand with confidence I didn't feel.

"Brenda" she said. Her shake was firm and her palm was dry and cool, quite unlike mine.

"You live around here?" she asked.

"A few blocks away. What about you?"

"I'm not from around here."

Her clipped response told me not to ask from where.

She pulled some blonde strands away from her face. Her skin was flawless. Once again she leveled that stare at me.

"I need to get out of here," she said, glancing around. "It's getting a little close in here."

I didn't know what had changed, but I wasn't going to argue.

"Are you going to join me or just sit with the rest and watch me walk outta here?"

My thoughts spun. "Where we headed?" I asked.

Holding my gaze, she said, "I'll tell you outside."

With that she slid off the stool and turned toward the door. When I stepped down off of mine the room once again went quiet. A path formed between us and the door. The billiard game stopped. I followed half a step behind her as we walked out into the heat.

"Let's go for a stroll in the park," she said when we got to the sidewalk.

We crossed the street and wandered into the park. It was nearly dark now. After a short walk, we were on a path through the trees. This was as close to a forest as one could get in the city. We neared a light pole and she stopped.

Turning toward me, she said, "You're intriguing. You don't say much either. But there is something about you that gets me hot."

I couldn't believe how forward this woman was. We stood facing each other. Her crimson lips were like magnets and I moved closer. Suddenly we joined in a passionate kiss. Nothing but our lips, and our tongues, touched. She let out a heavy sigh.

Breaking the kiss she stepped back a little. Her hand found mine and she pressed a key into my palm.

"I'm in the Biltmore, room 1242. Give me thirty minutes."

She spun on her heel and the click-click of her shoes faded into the darkness.

It was going to be a long thirty minutes.

I awoke to the sound of the door slamming against the wall. The lights came on, blinding me. My eyes adjusted and a black pair of orthopedic shoes swam into focus.

"Are you sleeping in here again, Mr. Silek?"

It was the cleaning woman for my office.

"Yeah, it's been another long day."

"You work too hard sir," she admonished.

The photos of the woman in red in the file on my desk made me wish I had been able to sleep just a few minutes longer.

Warm Enough?

Jim Topping

I checked once again to make sure all of the curtains in the kitchen were closed. The last thing I needed is one of the ladies from the local red hat society, the Stepford Wives of my complex, from peeking in and seeing Jasmine sitting immobile at the dining table. If they saw that, they'd start talking and asking questions and I don't need any of that.

It had been such a bummer of a day. It started out so well. Jasmine woke me up and was in one her moods. A short while later the sheets were on the floor on one side of the bed and we were on the floor on the other. Oh yeah! After a shower, together you know, doing our part to save water, she cooked me breakfast. I had just taken the third bite when it happened.

"How's your breakfast my Love?" Her sultry voice made me all warm inside, and she knew that.

"It's awesome Sweetheart, thank you." I said with a smile, captivated by her deep blue eyes.

"Is the syrup warm enough?... Warm enough?... Warm enough?"

Uh oh, I thought, her processor has crashed again. What a way to upset a perfect morning.

This has happened once before. She had locked up and began quoting dead English poets and drawing monkeys on the table with a pen she'd been using. Thankfully, no pen this time.

"Jasmine!" I said firmly. "Reset to zero load reset."

"Warm enough?... Warm enough? ...Warm enough?"

Now her right thumb began tapping rhythmically on the table.

This is bad, I thought. Thankfully after the last episode I had memorized the diagnostic procedures. The first step was to press the master reset button which was located on the back of her neck, just below the hair line. The default was it had to be held down for one second. However, I like kissing her there and an accidental press of the reset button tends to spoil the mood. So I'd had the parameter changed to five seconds.

As my lovely breakfast cooled and congealed, I got up and moved over behind Jasmine. I lifted up her lovely blonde locks and felt her rigid neck for the button, just below her silky soft skin and held it down for the requisite five seconds.

"Warm enough? ... Warm eno—"

Well, that took care of that problem. Now her processor would run a restart and IPL. However, one look at her face gave me disconcerting feelings. Normally during an IPL her eyes would be closed and her features relaxed. But this time they were wide open, staring at nothing. I went and retrieved my cell phone. Time to contact tech support. While on hold, awaiting a response, I got the laptop out and after opening the access cover next to her reset button, plugged in the HDMI cable. All at once I realized a piece of potentially distressing news. Jasmine is out of warranty. This could be expensive.

FALL

CONTEMPORARY FICTION

Drought

Terry Wellman

One

Stepping out of his car and walking toward the day's destination, he is hit with a stench like an invisible sentry guarding the enemy's encampment. Briny sweat, pungent body odor, stale urine, the aroma of cement baking in the sun, the sweet and sour mix of auto exhaust and low-grade pot, the sentry's warning is powerful. Associate Pastor Dex is not deterred. While in college, he had woken up in post-party wastelands emitting similar smells.

His brain loses the capacity to distinguish the various scents as he rounds the corner and passes through a chain-link fence. Just inside the fence, he sees a row of shopping carts, arranged in order of the height of the contents piled within, from lowest to highest. At the front of the line is a child-sized shopping cart from Trader Joe's. At the end, a behemoth from Costco, its wheel-locking mechanism dismantled and mockingly repurposed as a hood ornament. Facing out from the back of each basket are cardboard signs with various pleas: food, money, help, anything— each one punctuated with the ubiquitous, "God Bless." The sign in the child-sized basket is in child-sized handwriting, while the largest sign comes with Goliath all-upper case black magic marker lettering. The baskets are arranged with such care and precision, like exotic floats for the Rose Parade, that some camp member must be suffering from obsessive-compulsive disorder—or more likely using it as a way to cope with a life at the bottom.

The encampment comes into full view with a style that makes Brutalist architecture feel like Disneyland. Tents in various degrees of distress, stitched and duct-taped for success. A sea of blue tarps undulating in the Santa Anna winds. Lean-tos of various ingenuity with flattened cardboard box walls baked to a crisp, along with other distressed mothers of invention. The socks the cross-town Lutheran youth group gave out last winter were being used for their intended and other bizarre purposes. Regretting the lack of a cap or sunscreen, Dex sees a few bent heads scattered throughout the campground. With a beatific grin and letting the Spirit move him, the Lord's work begins.

"Everybody's journey is different," he says, using a stiff Bible as a sun visor. "You may have grown up hearing God's words and forgotten them. Or drugs, alcohol, crime, hate, have sanded away the words that should be etched on your heart."

He looks down and kicks a pebble out from between his left foot and leather flip flop, the jagged edge of his jeans kissing the ground. "You may have never even heard the Good Story before, the story of how Jesus Christ died for your sins. But with baptism in Christ and in the water, you will be saved."

"Hey, Mr. Preacher Man, don't you know we're in a drought? There ain't enough water down there to baptize my big toe," yells an unseen heckler. From underneath a tarp and cardboard structure with the Lutheran socks pinned up as curtains over a jagged window, a scratchy smoker's laugh morphs into a gravelly smoker's cough.

He scans the group of unwashed men for the smartass, but cannot locate the culprit among the many heads and faces that barely acknowledge his presence. Looking behind him at the dry Santa Ana River, Not even a little toe, really, he concedes.

Two

A different kind of drought had brought him to this homeless encampment in the shadow of Angels Stadium. "What good am I doing?" he sighed while sitting at his desk in the church office. This question had been pestering him like an unreachable itch throughout the first six months of his role as a young Associate Pastor at a growing non-denominational church in the most affluent areas of Orange County.

Sure, these souls likely needed saving, too, but Dex did not feel as if he were truly doing the Lord's work. Mother Theresa lived in Indian slums amidst the lowest caste, the Untouchables. Dex chaperoned the youth group's ski trip to Aspen. The money, houses, and vacations of many of the congregants were indeed impressive, but their level of giving was most certainly not. The Bible uses the tithe as an example, not a tithe of a tithe, he grumbled once to himself. How many mouths would a monthly payment on a new BMW feed? He did not want to do the math, eager to be rid of disillusionment and bitterness. He needed rain to drench the Dust Bowl his heart had become and transform it into a rainforest, a jungle, overgrowing, fertile, and abundant with life.

That was it. That was where he needed to go—out into the world, the desert, the jungle, the urban jungle. His mind raced back to the great missionaries he had read about while in seminary. Paul, of course, the greatest of them all. St. Patrick in Ireland. Taylor in China for over 50 years. Helen Roseveare in the Congo. This is what Jesus would really do. There were plenty of others to attend to the affluent flock and their First World problems.

All of the church staff was in the conference room celebrating another birthday with overpriced gourmet cupcakes. With a hollow promise of "Thanks, be there in a just a minute," Dex rose and snuck into the small chapel typically used for the more intimate "traditional services"— the ones without the rock band, choreographed light show, and Hollywood-esque video production. He checked his watch to make sure he would miss the daily crush of Land Rovers and Mercedes SUVs for the church's pre-school pick up and headed for the sanctuary. Grabbing a stiff, little-used Bible from the back of one of the pews, Dex opened the side door of the chapel and took the first step on his mission to the land of the lost, the forgotten, the most in need of compassion, healing and salvation.

Three

Dex pushes his blonde hair behind his ears and begins to comfort his first wayward soul. "We'll find you some water, my brother. No need to worry about that."

Because he grew up in the sunshine of Southern California and spent countless days at the beach, the abuse of the sun and seawater had given Dex permanent surfer hair. While in seminary, he was good-naturedly teased about the length of his hair by more conservatively coiffed seminarians. He joked that it gave him strength, like Samson, and that his policy was to refuse any alcoholic drinks from any woman named Delilah. While at the annual interdenominational softball tournament, he would quip with the Catholics that even washing with holy water could not save his hair.

"It doesn't matter where you've been, what you've done, God loves you. Jesus loves you. I love you."

A wounded Afghan war vet replies, "I love beer more than God loves me," punctuating his remark by throwing a beer can at Dex. Backwash and warm beer spill onto his red RVCA shirt, staining it between the V, like a chalice being filled.

He winces and looks at his shirt. "Oh, Lord, let this cup pass from me," he says to himself.

Undeterred, he continues. "Jesus died for your sins. He suffered so that you do not have to. All can be forgiven!"

But no one is listening.

A group of the drunks, the addicts, the "hobos," as he once heard a kid call them, the lost, and the forgotten are now mumbling and gathering near a red North Face tent with duct tape covering its rips and tears. There is devilish laughter now. Ominous. Menacing. Threatening. Nothing like his humor-studded sermons usually receive. He continues, louder.

"All you have to do is give your life over to Christ. Accept him as your savior. He will wash away your sins."

Two of the bigger men, one shirtless, and one—despite the heat— wrapped in a battle-worn green Army jacket favored by homeless everywhere, walk towards him. His heart jumps. The love of his profession soars. He thanks the Lord. He has made a difference. He opens his arms to receive them, sweat stains showing, feeling the developing sunburn on his neck begin to tingle.

When they reach the edge of his outstretched fingertips, Dex expects these lost souls to bow humbly and begin to experience the relief of giving one's burdens to Jesus. Instead, before he can even process an alternative, Dex is on the ground, gasping for air, unable to talk.

"That'll keep you quiet," the shirtless man declares.

Ignoring his partner's declaration, the man in the Army jacket launches a kick. Soon, more filthy hands and more soles of filthy shoes pummel him. It is as if his message is perverted and corrupted by ears deafened to hope and brains clogged by drugs. Between strikes, questions flood his waning consciousness. Why are they misunderstanding? What did I say wrong? What should I have said instead? I am not the one who is supposed to suffer and die for their sins. Christ already did that.

Dex briefly sees the flash of muted silver from a scuffed and worn army boot held together by duct tape as it traverses an arc on the way to a rib. Before the kick lands, Dex has an epiphany about how important duct tape is to the homeless. It should be given out along with food, socks and warm clothes. Is there a sermon in there? He wonders. But before he could think of ways to connect duct tape to salvation, the boot connects with his side, cracking one rib and then a second.

Through the new pain of a rock falling on his head, Dex's thoughts immediately race to Acts 7:57 and the stoning of Stephen, the first Christian martyr. Before he could get to verse 60 and say aloud like Stephen, "Lord, do not charge them with this sin," four men jerk him up by his arms and legs. Stephen, thinks Dex, while carried like a hog to a roasting pit; I really wanted to name our son Stephen or Timothy or one of the other great missionaries of the early Church. Instead, he gave in to his wife, Miranda, and his son Hayden has one of the myriad names that end with "aiden." How many in Hayden's pre-school class had a similar name? He begins, Brayden is one, Jayden is two, Caden is…

"Three!" With a heave and grunts, his captors toss him off the high bank of the river and down the cement incline, like a sack of potatoes being loaded on to a truck by migrant workers. As his body comically rolls and flops to the bottom, his thoughts, and organs, rumble and crash into each other like potatoes in a human sack.

His pulped body lands in an unnatural pose. His face rests sideways next to a mysterious car part in a shallow pool of water of suspicious and vile origins. Dex can't feel his swollen face, water now partially covering one inoperable eye. In what could be considered a miracle in this instance, the water stays clear of his nostrils. Partially opening his good eye, Dex realizes this is enough water to baptize a big toe. When he fully opens his one operable eye, he sees the bright sun shining on a glassy ocean. He draws what he hopes isn't one of his final breaths, takes in the salty air mixed with chemical undertones, and agrees when a seagull squawks to tell him that today would not have been good day for surfing either.

Later in the evening, after the camp's curiosity of a body in the cement river basin is overpowered by their desire of the next drink or fix, the sky opens, and the first drops of rain that will end one drought begin to fall. Hesitant at first, as if it knows better than to land in this sinful scene, the precipitation steadily increases and realizes that there is a job it must do.

Over the next several days, huddled inside their makeshift tents and lean-tos, the residents of the camp endure futile attempts to stay dry. Some wish for more duct tape, some for the way things used to be. The Santa Ana rises, and the current stirs, washing away their sins and carrying their sacrifice to the ocean.

Garbage

Summer Salmon

"This is how we live now," I said as I walked into my dad's home.

It wasn't a question any more. It was fact. I slammed the door behind me, the impact rattling the screen on the outside. There were stacks of books, papers, empty take-out containers and what I assumed was a pile of dirty underwear in the corner. But I wasn't going to go near it. It was worse than ever, and the smell made my eyes water.

My dad sat defiantly in his recliner, the one thing that wasn't stacked with shit. Or maybe he was just sitting on top of it.

"What's this 'we' crap?" He spat the words at me.

He flipped through the channels on the TV. He barely looked in my direction. Infomercials and Saturday morning cartoons were all the foil-covered antenna could pick up, since he had forgotten to pay the cable bill all year.

I shuffled through the garbage to the kitchen. I made sure to avoid the pile of soiled boxers. The kitchen wasn't any better. It was worse. The sink was full of filthy dishes and the garbage overflowed. Flies and other pests swarmed the area.

It had only been a month since my last visit. That time I had suited up in overalls, gloves, goggles, and a mask. I threw everything out as my dad screamed at me.

"I need that! Why are you such a bitch? That's just the "sell-by" date. It's still good for months after that!"

Many expletives flew from my sweet father's mouth. I kept my eyes on what needed to be done. It was hard to not engage, but there was no upside to fighting back with him.

My stress level rocketed to an all-time high every time I entered this house. One of these days my heart or my head would explode. I would collapse in a heap and no one would ever find me in the rubble. I would just be another pile of garbage in my dad's house.

He'd kick me each morning, moving my lifeless corpse out of the way so he could get to his morning coffee fix. The coffee maker was the one machine besides the TV that still worked in this house.

I pulled my turtleneck over my mouth and nose and opened the fridge. It muffled the smell some, but all the spoiled food on top of even older rotten things created a constant assault. I gagged inside my makeshift mask. There were so many containers of yogurt with puffed up lids. A few popped open as I dumped them into trash bag.

I replaced them with the fresh items I had brought. I had told myself that I wouldn't clean this time. I was just going to drop off the food and leave, but I started stacking plates and cups like the robot I turned into when I came here.

This had to be the last time, but I had made this declaration too many times to count, this lie that I told myself over and over. I postponed my visits a little longer each time, but guilt would take over. Especially when my brother Danny called and asked about Dad. Our last conversation went something like this:

"He's the same, Danny."

"You say that every time. Should I come out and check on him? Make sure you're doing what you say?"

What a bastard! I knew he would never come. He was too involved in himself and the world he created with his family far away from here. So I called his bluff.

"Would you, Dan? That'd be great."

There had been a long pause followed by:

"You know I can't." He stumbled over the words. "Soccer games and recitals coming up. Steffie would murder me if I missed any of them."

"Same old story, Danny boy. Can't wait to hear it again next month."

"You're such a bitch. You know that?"

"Yep. I'm the bitch who takes care of our father, and took care of our mother before she died, too. What a bitch!"

He didn't say anything, but I heard his breathing get faster and faster as he tried to control his anger. "I'll call you next week." The line went dead.

"Lookin' forward to it, dear brother," I spoke the words to dead air.

Next week would actually be another month before he remembered to call. It would be more resentments and new expletives we would hurl at each other.

I thought that older siblings were supposed to be the more responsible ones—the ones who took care of their parents when they got old and were unable to care for themselves. The youngest were supposed to be the selfish ones who got all the attention and didn't deserve it. We had it easier because the older ones wore our parents down; then we reaped the benefits and got away with murder.

I was the baby of our family, but apparently, I got all the maturity and compassion. I also got the cruel gene that made me feel like shit if I thought about myself before anyone else: the one that made me freeze when I had to make any decision about my life but allowed me to make the hard decisions about my mom's health needs. I was grateful for the strength when I had to sign the papers when there was no more hope that mom could stay with us anymore. Dad couldn't do it.

I leaned my head against the fridge, not caring what my skin was resting against. I was just feeding this madness. I was allowing him to keep hoarding trash. I knew it.

It was time to make the call. It was time to get some help for Dad.

I walked back into the living room. Dad had landed on an old Bugs Bunny episode. I sat on the couch near him and balanced precariously on a stack of clean newspapers.

I let him finish the episode. He was smiling and laughing. I hadn't seen that in ages. I realized I was smiling, too. In this moment I had my Dad back, if only for a few minutes. The tears came as I laughed with him.

It could wait a few minutes more.

On Comets and Chicken

May Grace

My mother's face is plastered on a billboard right outside my school. It makes me feel uneasy—as if I'm always being watched, always being judged. Her expression never falters, always picture perfect. Each tooth shines straight and white. I feel like I'm even held to her impossible standards at school, the place where I'm supposed to be myself and hold my own.

But still I am nameless, faceless. I am simply the daughter of Faline Palmeroy; no identity of my own is enough to shine through her shadow. Faline Palmeroy is my mother, the most successful newscaster in New York. Everybody knows Mom, and mostly everybody loves her. That peaceful love doesn't wash over to me, unfortunately. My school days are spent in solitude, and I sit as far away from the billboard as possible. Her cartoon eyes haunt me—they are deep-set and sad-looking, rimmed in powder blue eyeshadow. Without a conscience there is no hope—and I stand as nothing behind those blinking, bright eyes.

"Plum Palmeroy, you're going home early," said Miss Morris, my English teacher. I hated the way she'd announced it in front of the whole class. Now I had to walk past everyone to get to the door. I hated their taunting eyes. I despised the sound of their whispers, rolling in like wasps' wings at my feet.

"She thinks she's so damn cool, leaving early to go be on television. Well, she isn't, she's a dreadful witch!"

Imagine trying to blend in with a name like Plum. My parents were on something when they gave me that one. But a name of the strangest degree is only fitting for the heir of Cosmo Palmeroy. Cosmo's my father. He's been performing for years, music and poetry and pretty much anything else that will get people to look at him. I love my dad, but it's hard to when my teachers all fancy him. I'm glad I don't have any friends—I imagine they'd want to go over to my house solely to catch a glimpse of my father in the nude.

I walked to the front of Miss Morris' class, letting my long fringe flop in front of my face. Anything to avoid their glaring, staring eyes. Anything to spare being laughed at.

"Bye-bye, Plum. You enjoy the rest of your day, now," said Miss Morris, waving me off with one lilywhite hand.

I was running down the halls as fast as I could, desperate to be out of that place. The halls were empty, and that provided at least some peace of mind. I so hated to be looked at. That was the worst feeling in the whole world. As awful as it was when the kids at school did it, it was even worse when Mom and Dad's countless fans would leer at me with so much anticipation.

As if I could do anything worth staring at. It made me feel like a circus bear, feet flailing under fire. In a perfect world, I would be invisible, or at the very least, born to normal parents. I have everything against the extraordinary, and I have perfected the art of normalcy. I make sure to dress in one of three colors—black, grey, or brown. Bright makeup has no place on my ghost face. And so I lie in the shadows, desperate to evade. My parents wish I would be more like them—louder, bolder. In Dad's perfect world, I'd sing and dance and click my heels no matter where the hell I was or who the hell was watching. In Mom's, I'd keep all my hair out of my face and keep my eyebrows groomed. I'd look like a little china doll, not the bitter and spiky fruit for which I was named.

Mom stopped telling me when she was going to pick me up early from school, because she knew I'd fuss. I didn't want to go to dress fittings or meetings with her. I would rather work my part-time volunteer job at the hospital. Mom would die if she knew I, precious Plum Palmeroy, was helping the masses!

I was supposed to be doing better things with my time, like modeling. Mom paid a hefty sum to have me trained after school at Mistress Ursula's modeling academy, but I never went once. The thought of standing there in my underwear while Mistress Ursula heckled me was enough to turn me white as a sheet. I got a job volunteering at the hospital instead. We have to wear candystriper dresses, but I don't mind them. I blend in with all the other girls, laughing creatures that sometimes go camping together on the weekends. The hospital is the only place in existence where people are too busy to assign me the role of Plum Palmeroy. I'm just Plum, who brings food into rooms and chats to patients and helps them.

My sickest patient is Martin La Croix. He's seventeen, just like me. But he's got leukemia. Mom and Dad have a thing with the La Croixes—I'd be in such trouble if they knew I willingly looked after Martin's health. Mom is jealous of Martin's mother, Eleanor. That's where the whole debacle comes from, Mom's insecurity. Eleanor is beautiful, in an undead kind of way. She is the opposite of Mom in every visible outcome— Mom is petite, every feature of hers is small and soft. Her cornsilk blonde hair is short and her eyes are bright and blue. Eleanor is dark, dark, dark. Her hair is black and straight, and I don't think she has ever cut it. Her eyes are so saturated in pigment that you can't see her pupils against them. But I like Martin. I feel bad that he's dying and can't do anything to stop it. He and I both know he's good as gone, but we don't say goodbye. It's always a "see you later."

I always get out of Martin's room before his family comes in, though. Eleanor and her husband, Vincent, despise me. They've never met me, but per usual, what I am is determined by the ones who have come before me. My job puts me on the line—puts Martin on the line. But I am a doormat in every other color—I will not give up the hours of my day where I am free to just be.

"Plum, you're so slow, sweetheart!" I trudged out to the parking lot, and Mom beckoned me towards the car with flippant manicured hands. She had a tulle scarf tied under her neck, keeping her hair rollers in place. She still looked glamorous though—lips greased in red and eyes spackled in blue. She beeped the horn on her car, a custom-made turquoise Lambo. "Come on, Plum!"

I got in the car with a blank scowl on my face. Mom was blaring one of Dad's embarrassing songs, per usual. "We're going to be late to my appointment, doll, but it's ok. Such a shame you'll miss your lesson at Mistress Ursula's today."

I nodded, feigning regret. "Oh, rats!"

"Look at what Mommy says, P," Mom pointed to her own billboard as we burned out of the school parking lot. Underneath the huge picture of her, there was big purple text, reading FALINE PALMEROY'S BIG SHOW: WHERE STARS ARE MADE.

"I don't wanna be a star, Mom."

"Being difficult and obstinate is a right of teenage passage. I know you're only resisting because it's what Daddy and I want for you. But you'll come around, won't you?" Mom smacked her gum loudly, blowing it up in a big bubble. I leaned further back in my seat.

"Please don't call him Daddy."

"Oh please, Plum. You're so bothered by everything!"

She tweaked my arm with a grin on her face. I only sighed.

I really wish Dad would give the whole music thing up. He's had his fun, but he's forty-five now. There's no need for him to be wearing skin-tight jeans in front of thousands and singing about women's bodies. He's been in the limelight for twenty years, and it's time to retire the act. The first thing you see when you look at him is all his long, permed hair. He totally loves to be loved, and people adore him. It's direly bothersome that my teachers grew up with their hands down their pants at the sight of my father. What kind of respect does that leave me with?

I'm a bastard child, born out of wedlock. Mom and Dad never got married, because they're too glamorous for that. They both make loads of money and don't see a need in sharing it. Mom changed her last name though because she wanted to put together her perfect, plastic family, the kind that sing together and wear matching suits. That couldn't happen if her name wasn't the same as Dad's. She calls it a "forever arrangement," pretty much a marriage, minus the sanctity. Mom would soil everything white and lacy. Vincent and Eleanor La Croix are married, and Mom thinks they're lame for it.

I don't think Mom should even care. If she spent less time thinking about what everyone else was doing, maybe she wouldn't find so much fault in herself. The La Croixes have a deep, blood-red love, and I'm convinced they have spent lifetimes together before appearing in this form. Mom thinks they're vampires. Vincent does look a bit like a bat, and that same snouty face has been passed on to his sons, Martin and Lancelot. Lancelot La Croix is Martin's twin, but he makes up in vulgarity where Martin falters. Lancelot's a bully, plain and simple. Eleanor is filthy rich off her clothing label, Scarlet Ibis, and as the head of house, Vincent reeks with black power. That's the difference between Lancelot and me—I wish nobody knew who my parents were. There isn't a day in class that goes by when he lets us forget who his are.

Mom's appointment was a dress fitting at her seamstress's office. As it gets closer to the Night of the Stars, which is an awards ceremony put on by the rich and affluent of New York, Mom pulls out all her stops. Every year, Eleanor wins the best-dressed award and it makes my mother's blood boil. Mom refuses to wear Scarlet Ibis dresses, refuses to be caught dead in Eleanor's prints. But I like them—they are stitched in gold threading and blue flowers.

There was only so much of Mom's boasting to the seamstress I could handle without wanting to tear my brains out. "You see, Flora, I just can't find any dress that works my figure how I want it!"

Flora nodded, her waxy old face worn ragged. "I made your dress custom, Faline."

"And don't you forget it," said Mom. Her dress was super short and hot pink. She resembled a flamingo at the best of times, but now, it was just too easy to laugh at her. Although she is difficult, I love my mother, and I admire her ability to stand out. That's something I could never do. Mom made a name for herself, and that's a pretty big accomplishment for a woman in this world. I'd like to do that too, but of course, the name was given to me when I was born. Palmeroy. Been here before.

I pushed my thick, short hair behind my ears, sitting awkwardly in Flora's dressing room. "Does Miss Plum have a dress as well?" I shook my head.

"Nope."

"Wrong," said Mom, smiling at herself in the mirror. She always used her billboard face in public, bright white and enchanting. "Of course you have a dress, P. You're going to be a stargirl at this year's Night of the Stars ceremony."

The Night of the Stars is old news. The same people have always won the same awards. Mom gets best business mogul, Eleanor gets best-dressed and Dad gets best icon. I've never won anything, and that embarrasses my parents greatly. The little La Croix rat boy, Lancelot, wins every year for innovation. He's never innovated anything. He simply is the child of a celebrity with the balls to own it—and if that's not what the people of New York want on stage, I don't know what is. I don't even get the point of celebrating all this—it's not like they're real accomplishments, anyway. It's like a pat on the back to the insecure adults that own us kids, the ones that rule the streets. I hope I'm never that old, that desperate. I hope I feel good enough within myself that I don't need to look outside for validation.

"What's a stargirl?"

Even the term seemed horrifying. I peered at Mom uneasily.

"You'll be posed by one of the tables, and you'll present awards. All your little friends would go wild for this opportunity, Plum. You have so much privilege, and all you ever do is complain."

I complain because the only privileges I am allotted have no place in my world.

"I don't really want to be a stargirl, and I don't have any friends," I said.

"Oh, you! Difficult, difficult, difficult, isn't she, Flora?" Mom laughed as she always did. She always laughed over my complaints, perhaps to convince herself that I was only joking, that I wasn't sure enough of myself to know what I wanted.

My mother was a confused nut at seventeen, who looked to others to make her choices for her. Because of this, she assumes I am the same, a carbon copy. I am so far from her that we stand in separate worlds. I wish I could talk to Mom, more than anything. I wish she'd hear me. Wish she wouldn't always be laughing.

I thought of my shift at the hospital going untouched. What if someone needed me? What if they threw out my dress, with its red stripes the color of blood? I had the chicken shift today—it was a Tuesday, and that was the day they made fried chicken for the patients. I'd never been scheduled to work the kitchen on a Tuesday, but today, I was. I'd always wanted to do that.

"I left some of my books at school, Mom," I said, looking longingly out of Flora's window. "I'm going to go get them."

That's how to speak to Mom. I can't ask to get my books. I have to stand as tall as I can and let her know I'm going, whether she likes it or not. The only thing I have no control over is my presence at events— she'd handcuff me to her if need be. I've never missed one Night of the Stars in all my seventeen years of life.

"School so doesn't matter, Plum, but off you go. You don't even have to go to university, but you want to! What kind of a perturbed child..." Mom was already ranting to Flora, forgetting I'd even spoken in the first place.

I was bounding down the road on foot towards the hospital with a deep, smug feeling in my chest. I ran the rest of the way, as I was already going to be late. I threw my dress on, tossed my lanyard over my head, and turned around to greet my manager, Dr. Collins. He's pretty young to be a doctor, and he's nice to all of us. If I were going to date someone, I'd like to go out with Dr. Collins.

"I'm sorry I was late, Dr. Collins."

"You're here, Plum, that's what matters," he said, putting his hand on my shoulder comfortingly. I let my fringe fall over my face again, obscuring my blush.

"Has somebody already taken my chicken shift?" I could hear sounds of laughter coming from the kitchen and thought of the barrels of batter to be stirred up and the spices to be thrown.

It was a field day of artistic duality in there, and I'd missed it.

"Yes, some of the other girls stepped in to cover your shift. You'll work it again in six weeks, don't you worry. Now go down and grab some food for your assigned patients today, Ms. Potter, Mr. Friedman and Martin La Croix."

I walked into the kitchen with my head hung. Six weeks? Mom's ideas always got in the way of my plans, the things I knew I wanted for myself. It made me feel stupid, like my say is nothing. Like I'd never dictate my own life. I'd be ninety, and still Plum Palmeroy, daughter of Faline and Cosmo—a girl so shy she never was an heir.

One of the girls cooking the chicken paused to hand me a plate of food.

"You're alive!"

"Unfortunately," I said. "This came out a bit rubbery," she giggled, "you ought to cook it next time, Plum! I nearly burned the place down." She and the other girl kept laughing, giggling, over burnt chicken and covered shifts. They seemed carefree and proud, and I admired them for it.

I carried the tray of food into Martin's room first, because he was my favorite patient. Ms. Potter had dementia and could never remember who I was or what I was doing, even though I saw her every day. Mr. Friedman liked to yell about politics and liked to yell at me. Martin was too sick to say much, and he had a little music box by his bedside. It would tinkle and flow with a Christmas song while a miniature ceramic bear danced on one foot. I found myself coming back into Martin's room not to refill his water or help him to the bathroom, but to hear his music box. It made me think of the idyllic times of my childhood—how fast those years had flown past.

The chicken was burned black, and the asparagus hung like limp, thin hair off the sides of the plate. There was some sort of sauce, but it was too thick to be ranch and too thin to be gravy. I shuddered at the presentation.

I pushed Martin's door open and set the dinner tray on his nightstand, fumbling around on the wall for the light. My eyes glanced at Martin's bed, and I noticed a figure crouched down on the floor. The figure turned to stare back at me, and we gasped at one another.

He dug in his pocket and grabbed something.

"Stupid Plum Palmeroy, got off school early to come work here?" Lancelot La Croix growled, throwing a rock at my head. I dodged, and it dented the wall. I took my dumb little hat off and set it by Martin's plate.

"It's my job, Lancelot. Just leave me alone."

"You have no right to be in my brother's room," snarled Lancelot, getting up. He walked closer to me, his fists balled. He had bones like an animal, and his hair could have used a good wash. He had frog's eyes. His whole face was just a monstrous mishmash of the worst creatures ever formed, creepy toads and infectious bats.

Lancelot had a big golden ring on every finger, and they shined with heinous potential. I could see my own scared face in the reflections of the facets. I took another step towards the door. Just slide away, P, just flood out the door. I was almost gone when I saw Martin reach out for his dinner plate, desperately. I handed him the tray and placed the plastic fork in his hand. It was my job, after all. If Lancelot was going to give me trouble, I could get Dr. Collins. But I didn't want to look weak. I was weak at school and weak at home. This was supposed to be my place, but I guess even that had been taken from me.

"I work here. I can be anywhere on the premises. If anyone's violating laws here, Lancelot, it's you. You tried to assault me with that rock—" my voice was shaky, and his face was mean. Poor Martin had slipped out of focus, gray fingers hardly holding his fork.

"Assault you? You have such a superiority complex, Plum. You think you're so much better than everyone because your parents are Cosmo and Faline Palmeroy, but guess what? No one cares. Your mom's a slut and your dad's washed up."

He was such a pest, and an idiotic one, too. I was nothing like him, using my parents' names for personal gain. That was some shoddy self-reflection if I'd ever seen it.

"Eat shit. That's you!" I said. "You come in late to class every day, don't do anything, but you still come out with an A. You make sure the teachers fear you. You get off on fear, you love having your ego praised and stroked. You're not God almighty. And don't you ever let me catch you with my parents' names in your mouth or I'll punch your yellow teeth down your throat."

Lancelot tucked his dirty hair behind his ears. "Do you wanna fight?"

"Lancelot!" Martin cried, "could I just eat in peace?"

"Sorry, Marty. I'm going to speak with the doctor so we can get you a new aide. You shouldn't have to see her face every day. That would make me want to be dead, yuck!"

I stood still in the corner, glaring at him. Why on Earth had my position at school overflowed to my second life? I was nothing, I remembered, but if I let someone as foolish as Lancelot La Croix take away my freedom, I was just plain stupid. I gnashed my feet into the carpet.

"It's my choice," said Martin, "and I think Plum does a great job."

"The medicine's rotted your brain," Lancelot snarled.

"He gets to choose, not you. I know you're sad, as you always get whatever you want. But please, Mr. La Croix, with all due respect, go to hell."

"I'll come back at 5, Marty. She just pisses me off." Lancelot picked up his skateboard and charged for the door, purposely slamming into me so hard that it hurt.

I slapped him in the face, leaving big welts from my nails.

"You don't charge at me, kid."

Lancelot bit his lip, bringing his hand over the red mark on his cheek. "You're a fucking barnacle, Plum. If you think you can fight me, bring it on."

"I have no want nor need to fight you."

Lancelot tossed back his greasy hair. "Well, unless you want me telling my parents that you're working for Martin, I'm gonna need something from you. Fortunately for the both of us, I have no desire to kiss you. I want you to nominate me for an award at the Night of the Stars."

I'd put myself through all of this just to cook fried chicken. I hadn't even been allowed that small wish, and now, the flesh was charred and cancerous.

I said nothing and looked back at Lancelot's mean, ugly face.

Mom and Dad would kill me if they knew I was caring for the La Croix boy. But this hospital was my world, and there was no way I was going to give it up. I'd let Lancelot blackmail me, I'd give him another award. I felt as if Mom and Dad were watching from the windows, heartbroken at my treachery. But I got a little closer to Lancelot anyways, my feet feeling heavy as they moved.

"Fine," I scowled, extending my hand to meet his.

It was a business deal, not a peace offering. It was no call of young mutiny.

Maybe he'd die. Maybe I'd never have to do it. But as I took my hand away from his, I realized I'd already made a mistake I could never take back.

WINTER

POETRY

1975

Ris Fleming-Allen

Godzilla rides his new bike to Tokyo,
rings the doorbell and runs back
off the porch, skipping foot to foot
in new corduroy bellbottoms
so excited to show Mothra
the training wheels came off

The Anthropocene

Ris Fleming-Allen

Take any metaphor, euphemism, simile or adjective you like, but how we live is how we live. The sun comes up, the sun goes down. Food goes in, poop comes out.

Life might be a song, but sometimes that song is too hard with too many notes as the king told Mozart, and you need a few extra hands on the piano. Or gurney.

Fuck Pinterest and Instagram. It won't be a stylish marriage, but goddammit, we'll make it last until the sun goes down, the food stops going in and extra hands carry us home.

A Bubble-durban and Tea-mar-two-knees

or

The Drinking Songs of My Childhood

Ris Fleming-Allen

Inkin' blinkin'
I been thinkin'
let's rush the growler
with the little man's can
but not on Sunday
when we hunt for beer
that tastes like wine
oh my god, it's turpentine

Crimson Rose

Vincent Scambray

A crimson rose, your favorite flower.
Running red rose petals, tracing that path,
Falling, hour after hour.
I'll plant you when I'm mounted up that hill,
My jealous care incurred your wrath,
And trace back my path from mountain still,
With pricks of thorns upon my fingers,
And carry with me my heavy heart,
Your crimson blood upon my sheets, it lingers,
Dark shadows of what has become our end,
True to the old adage,
Every murderer is someone's old friend.

Ephemera

Thom Kerr

The gentle hum of bees fills the air. I sing to them as I slog along the fence guarding Farmer Morton's trees. I listen and watch them work. They are tireless. Blossoms perfume the air and each day is a little warmer, a little more fragrant than the day before. Singing is the secret. My mother never sang out here and although her honey was sweet, mine always seems sweeter. I sing with my daughter in anticipation. Where my voice is gruff and low, hers carries the timbre of a violinist, sul tasto: ephemeral, light, airy, delicate and fleeting. Her voice will blend in harmony with the sounds of the workers.

The hives are abuzz
it's almost time to harvest.
Three frames from a hive
produces about ten pounds
that tastes as sweet as it looks.

Fragments

Vincent Scambray

Too many fragments
Of my spirit
I have scattered
Amongst these streets
Too many are the
Children of my longing
I cannot withdraw from them
Without a burden and an ache
Wandering to a place
We will never meet
Where my voice carries my words
But it's my lips that give it wings
To these things
To these things

The Future of the Poetic Arts

Terry Wellman

In the future, crowds will gather excitedly to hear his poems
That transform and transport and transfix.
Tickets for his readings will sell for multiples of face value.
Corporations will have skyboxes full of bigwigs.
Millions will watch the worldwide broadcasts.

He will be the new rock star, the new celebrity.
Rappers and songwriters will fail to imitate him.
Actors will ache to give life to his words.
Chefs will weep in efforts to translate his beauty to the plate.

He will be the undisputed master of all the classic forms:
His limericks will be mimicked in comedy clubs.
His imagistic poetry will replace photography.
His pastoral poems will calm the fevered and angry.

His sonnets will make Shakespeare's Dark Lady seem chaste.
The Greeks' epic heroes will humbly give up their quests to listen to his.
Emily Dickinson's hope will pluck its feathers in despair.

After warming up the fervent crowd with a few haikus and a short ballad,
He will ask the adoring stadium crowd, "Let's see, what next?"
Without a doubt some drunken yahoo, with a lighter, will yell,
"Free verse!"

Midsummer Night Special

Vincent Scambray

I have never known such an all consuming delight,
I am an addict for her body.
I think of nothing but her sex, her breasts, her mouth,
The slight folds where her buttocks meet the back of her legs.
A light whip,
To bind her.
When I am not with her
I live,
I plan,
I think,
Only for the time of our next meeting.
I am bound.
I am a pig, routing deeper and deeper into that muck,
For the last tantalizing morsel which just eludes me.
I am an enthusiast of degradation,
And the most rank of indulgences.
I have a nose for it much like the connoisseur has for fine wine,
I more than tolerate my decadent and perverse skill.
I am a slave to appetite,
I am obsessive,
I am compulsive,
I am going deeper and faster,
I am drinking it all in,
I am a sadist,
I am a masochist,
I am an addict,
I am alive!

Sally the Stripper

Thom Kerr

Something whimsical written at an OC Writers Guild meeting in 2014

Sally the Stripper beckoned
The old man to the stage.
He shook his head
"I got stiff ole bones, on account of my old age."
Sally was insistent,
"I've seen stiff old bones before,
It's what I do. It's who I am
It's what I'm up here for."

Two topless girls came over
And helped him climb the stair.
He clutched his chest, fell to his knees
Gave everyone a scare.

Sally dropped on top of him
She started CPR.
A call was made to 911
By the girl behind the bar.

When the paramedics got there
He waved them all away.
"Come back in just a minute please,
She's about to make my day."

Stella

Thom Kerr

Stella got back from Vietnam and everything changed
All her boyhood things went from her mother's house into
the trash or the Goodwill
Everything
except one photo of her, as Steve, in the Rio Grande, that she kept
because her dad had taken it
The water had been muddy that day, just after the storms
Her dad had snapped the picture right before he jumped in to join her
They swam together for hours

She found a doctor in Chicago who was willing to 'doctor'
the paperwork for the VA
She tried to forget all about South East Asia,
but it was tough
She wrote a "One Woman" play about a girl with a vegetable fetish
It sucked, but got rave reviews and ran for seven years, off Broadway

She had simple tastes
Nothing ostentatious
Most of the Money from the play went to veterans organizations
She kept some of it though, and bought a spread in the high desert
She wrote poems there
She scattered them to the prairie winds
Or tacked them to the walls of the shack until the ink faded from the
sun,
or the wind spirited them away

On her last birthday she dug out the photo of Steve in the river and
laid it on the table
She wished she had a photo of her dad, she thought
as she chambered a round in her .45

No one heard the ending
No one felt a thing
No alarm was sounded
Stella lived on her terms
– as volatile as they may have been

Only one regret
The Corps and Vietnam

Maybe that was two, but she really didn't care anymore.

Sterling-Rock Falls, Illinois

Ris Fleming-Allen

I learned to knit
on gasoline coffee vigils
outwaiting death
in this charnel town
full of memories and rage
enough to fire the smelters
along the river
long since torn down
eagles nest there now

Trying to Take Over the World

Ris Fleming-Allen

It's tough to be what you really are
while battered by rules
from thou shalt not steal
to do not eat this giraffe.

Avoid alliteration, do not litter
do not pull, do not press
the history eraser button
foghorns are not toys.

Gravity is pretty definite
about which end goes up
but the USPS will not ship
my brand new nuclear warhead
neither will FedEx.

When Words Fail

Terry Wellman

I forgot to my bring my receipts,
But not one of these words works.
There are too many repeats.

The adjectives are lame.
I have never heard of the nouns,
And the adverbs have no game.

I most certainly did not want
Onomatopoeia, gubernatorial,
Lugubrious, or Vermont.

My purchase I do rue.
I threw some verbs against the wall.
And stomped on a few.

I cannot pronounce words 23, 47, 54.
These are all useless.
I might as well speak in semaphore.

I'll complain about this on Reddit.
What?
Yes. I'll take store credit.

Oh…what aisle for the flags?

Authors

P.G. Badzey

P.G. Badzey combines his love for epic fantasy with his background in the engineering profession to create the Grey Riders series of novels (*Whitehorse Peak, Eye of Truth, Helm of Shadows and Assassin Prince*). Inspired by authors like JRR Tolkien, CS Lewis and Terry Brooks, P.G. Badzey provides a unique perspective, crafting stories of faith combined with a science-based magic system. His short stories have been published by *Dragonlaugh*, an on-line fantasy humor magazine, and his novels have been featured in *Midwest Book Review*. A member of the OC Writers Guild, he has appeared at multiple Indie Author events and has taught seminars on Fantasy Writing at OC Libraries.

Terry Black

Terry Black has written for film and television, as well as cartoons, comic books, videogames, and short stories. He writes a monthly column for the Oracle, the Newsletter of Orange County Mensa, filled with tales of his own crazy adventures. He lives in California with the reincarnated Queen of Atlantis and two mostly black cats, who bring him much-deserved bad luck.

You can find Terry at *terryblackmysterywriter.com, www.orangecoast.com/author/terry-black, www.imdb.com/name/nm0085535*

Lisa Congdon

Lisa Congdon traveled coast to coast before finally putting down roots in beautiful western North Carolina, where she and her characters explore the scenic mountain ranges together. Lisa understands that it takes hard work, sacrifice and often sheer determination to write a best-selling novel. More than anything, it requires passion for creating a well-told story that truly captures one's imagination while bringing to life what's possible. Her non-fiction books and romance novels can be found on *Amazon.com*.

Ris Fleming-Allen

Ris Fleming-Allen is not a starving poet as she graciously accepts a steady paycheck to design advertising. Ris has been published through various poetry contests and anthologies in the Midwest and Southern California. With support from the OC Writers Guild, she is attempting prose.

May Grace

May Grace is a high-school student who enjoys reading, writing, and drawing. Her stories and poems have been published in educational literary magazines. She writes genres such as young adult, romance, and drama. May lives in Southern California, works at a clothing store and plans to begin a literary magazine with a friend. She is inspired by stories such as *The Lovely Bones* and *Wuthering Heights*. Her story in this anthology tells the tale of children from rival families thrown together through blackmail. Currently, May is editing her first novel, which she began writing at 15. She hopes to study writing in college.

Anita Grazier

For most of her writing life, Anita Grazier shared her stories with no one but her mother, who was bound by parental duty to proclaim the tales extraordinary! With the encouragement of good friends in the OC Writers Guild, Anita finally decided to expand her audience.

Anita has no current plans to write the great American novel (or even a mediocre American novel) but you can find bits and pieces of her writing at *afterthecommercial.wordpress.com* and *storieswithoutend.wordpress.com*

Jennifer Hedgecok

Jennifer Hedgecock earned a Ph.D. in English from Michigan State University. Her publications include *The Femme Fatale Motif in Nineteenth Century British Literature* (Cambria Press), *"William Blake and The Road to Hell: Demystifying the Cultural Iconoclasm of the Hells Angels"* (Oxford UP), and *"The Black Leather Motorcycle Queen and the Passion of Madness"* (Oxford UP). Her upcoming publication *The Cultural Representations of Medusa* will be in print late 2019 (Routledge Publishers).

Leigh Mary

Leigh Mary has been a member of the OC Writers Guild since February 2013. She has been published in many poetry anthologies. After nearly twenty years in Seattle, she currently lives in Orange County, California. Works in process include two upcoming projects: *Deserved* and *The Presence*.

You can follow Leigh at *nyleighmary.wordpress.com*. Leigh would like to thank RJ for reminding her what she is passionate about in life.

Thom Kerr

Armed with plenty of pencils, a notebook, coffee, a laptop computer and a slow gait, Thom Kerr likes to make things up and write them down for his own amusement. He smiled when he first discovered that others can enjoy the same stuff that he does.

As a submarine veteran and a cancer survivor, Thom's view can sometimes be skewed, but he has had his work published in *Veterans Voices*, Dec. 2017, and *Vita Brevis Poetry Magazine* among others. He writes regularly for The New, Unofficial, On-line Writer's Guild, and Carrot Ranch Literary Community. Learn more at his blog, *tnkerr.wordpress.com*.

Christine O'Connor

Christine O'Connor was the U.S. Correspondent for several international magazines focusing primarily on architecture, construction and business, publishing more than three hundred articles. She also won four National Federation of Press Women Awards—three for features and one for a non-fiction book. Christine has been a magazine editor, copy editor, technical writer, book reviewer, staff feature writer, ghost writer, educator and poet.

Christine was born in Dorset, England and has been living in the U.S. since 1978.

Summer Salmon

Summer Salmon was born and raised in Northern California, but escaped to the grey skies of the Pacific Northwest where she met her wonderfully supportive husband. Always up for an adventure, they headed south for a little slice of the beach life in beautiful Southern California. Summer writes fiction and screenplays full time and will be publishing her first romance novel, set in the world of baseball, very soon. When she's not writing, she enjoys reading romance novels, binge-watching Downton Abbey over and over and finding the perfect London Fog tea latte. Summer can be found at @buffysol on Twitter and Instagram.

Vincent Scambray

Vincent Scambray has a Bachelors in Communication from University of California Santa Barbara. He began writing creatively on March 31, 2016. Vincent is working toward building his collection of poetry, prose, and short stories, and has a book in the works. Stay tuned.

James Topping

Writing became one of James Toppings's passions after scratching out the beginning of a novel on a legal pad. Years later, the writing got more serious and he joined his first writing group. The group subsequently folded, and in mid-2013 James found his way to the OC Writers Guild. That long not-so-lost novel is still a dream in the making. Meanwhile, newly married James is exploring and growing his writing by working on short stories and technical writing. Some of James' work can be found in his blog at *jtoppingblog.wordpress.com*

Terry Wellman

Terry Wellman was a classically-trained child prodigy on the Theremin. However, before Terry could become internationally famous for his skill and artistry, a rival thereminist stole both of Terry's hands and replaced them with a pair of salad tongs and a muddy brown shoe. The lack of proper hands made life difficult for Terry thereafter. His job as an apprentice mohel lasted only one day. With little hope and living off government disability checks, Terry spent his days in the local library consuming the works of Karl Marx, Dr. Seuss, Woody Allen and an owner's manual from a 1974 Datsun. Thus inspired, Terry picked up pen in his salad-tong hand and begin to write barely legible stories and poems. In time his handwriting approved. His most legible writing, though with a few mud stains, can be found at *40footbuffet.com*. Terry lives in Orange County, Calif. In his free time he volunteers as a medical cadaver at UCI Medical School.

Acknowledgements

The OC Writers Guild would like to thank the Newport Beach Public Library. We would also like to thank the Third Street Writers for selecting most of the pieces featured in this anthology through a blind reading process. Their support and partnership made this anthology possible.

Contributing members of the OC Writers Guild

Top, Left to right: Ris Fleming-Allen, Vincent Scambray, Christine O'Connor, P.G. Badzey, Terry Black, Leigh Mary, Summer Salmon, James Topping, Anita Grazier

Below, left to right: Lisa Congdon, May Grace, Jennifer Hedgecock, Thom Kerr, Terry Wellman

47935748R00084

Made in the USA
San Bernardino, CA
15 August 2019